THORNS AT SUNRISE

Star-Crossed Fairy Tales
Book Two

Janeen Ippolito

Line editing and proofreading: Sarah McConahy
Formatting: Sarah Delena White
Cover Design: Yvonne Less of Art 4 Artists

To Heidi, for always encouraging dragons,
and to Lady Kaz, for making such a short life so significant and furrific.

Thorns at Sunrise

You offer the dreams and the safety of night

All cares and concerns

Vanished from sight

Yet beware, my dear

Of the thorns at sunrise

You say we are destined for goodness and joy

All madness and mayhem

Will never destroy

Yet always, my dear

There are thorns at sunrise

You claim we could stop that which is foul

All horrors and harbingers

No longer despoil

Yet remember, my dear

There are thorns at sunrise

And try as you may

And try as you might

You can never remove them

Would you condemn yourself

Ever to fight

Against the thorns at sunrise?

A sacrifice made

A sacrifice lost

A terrible end

An immeasurable cost

When the thorns

Came

At sunrise

CHAPTER ONE

Her imaginary friend was playing a new trick on her. This time, she would discern his meaning.

Usilea set down the quill on the paper, frowning at the words mocking her from the page. She pressed her lips together in thought. Thorns at sunrise? What could it mean? What was her mind trying to tell her?

"What do you think of my riddle?"

As usual, the voice didn't come from within her mind directly, but somewhere outside. Yet were she to glance around, all she would perceive is the vaguest sensation of shadow and soul in the periphery of her vision.

And so, she refrained from looking. Instead, she focused on the words she had written, words he had spoken into her mind at some point in the night.

I think ... you're afraid.

"And what am I afraid of, goldenbird?" Amusement teased the edges of his words. She had known her friend was a male since the first time they had met, whenever that had been. Sometime after her

sixth year. *"Tell me, you who know me so well."*

I know you as well as I might any figment of my imagination.

"Likewise. That is not the answer to the riddle."

A sigh escaped her. Usilea leaned back in her cushioned chair and rubbed the tense area around her eyes. *You are afraid of being lost. You are afraid of being found. You are afraid of darkness, and you are afraid of light.*

No answer came from the voice in her mind. A faint smile curved her lips. He only withdrew like that when she was right and he was bewildered. She had learned that pattern over the years as they had conversed. He liked keeping his mysteries, while he equally delighted in unveiling the mysteries of others. A curious behavior for her imaginary friend.

A strange, stabbing sensation pierced through her musing.

What did it imply about her that her closest friend wasn't real?

I am a lonely person. That is all it could be.

Usilea turned back to her neatly organized papers, finding an older parchment worn with years. Other poems were there, as well as drawings and paintings from dreams they had shared. Had she been a traditional Mender, she might have believed she was contacting her soul-partner. All Menders had one. Due to their gift of empathically Receiving the injuries and ailments of others, and then healing from the wounds themselves, the soul bond was vital for mutual support and strength.

But Usilea wasn't a traditional Mender. She was a healer of other Menders, which meant her fate could very well be different from that of her brother and his destined love, Renna. And Mender connections started during the night hours when both individuals were sixteen or older. She and her friend had been interacting at various times throughout both night and day since she was six. All of this meant she could not be speaking with her spouse.

Instead, it means I am slightly disturbed and creative enough to make my own company.

"*No, you are not.*"

A quiet laugh escaped her. *It is oddly pleasant that I continue to dispute myself about this.*

"*I am many things, goldenbird, but I am not of your imagination.*" How firm he could be when he was insistent. Perhaps this was her own mind as well. Others had said she had much resolve.

You have not proven otherwise. She kept her mental voice light, teasing. Whoever this figment was, he enjoyed debate, but only to a certain extent. *Come now, let's change the subject, shall we?*

The shadowy image at the corner of her eyes wavered in irritation. "*Only if you understand that you are not mentally disturbed. You are incredible.*"

I could be both. More of that teasing, of the sort she only enjoyed with him because he had started it so long ago. *Calm yourself, clever boy. Whoever, whatever you are, I am glad for your presence.*

Indeed, she always had been. Especially when, at age twelve, her parents had begun training her in their terrible practices with Menders. When she learned of how Menders had been placed into slavery under the guise of religious piety, consigned to Receive from the wealthy elite until the Menders died young due to overuse of their healing gift. When she had learned of the cremations, the grinding of Mender bones into powders, and the other desecrations the former queen and king had committed to further their own lifespans.

All of this horror Usilea had borne in silence, forbidden to tell her brother Jaric. She only had her devotion to the Eternal and the comfort of her imaginary friend. Often, he would tell a joke or distract her with a riddle or reference the Holy Scrit. Sometimes, he would help her plan out strategies for her takeover of her parents' rule. Sometimes he was merely … present. The knowledge of his existence, even if unreal, was air in her lungs when she couldn't find the hope to breathe.

It was even more, now that she was queen. The Mender queen, as far as her people knew. She and her family didn't deem it necessary for her subjects to know the details of her unique gifting. It was enough that she was a Mender. The people saw her and her brother Jaric as beacons of hope. Though they had been born from the horrific actions of their parents ingesting Mender remains, the siblings had overthrown their parents, ended the enslavement of Menders, and offered themselves as humble civil servants.

Now, two years later and with the birth of her niece and nephew, the past was finally fading. At least for others. She still had to prove herself to be more than her parents' legacy. She must be the queen her people deserved, while having so few to guide her.

If she believed in fairness, it would have seemed very unfair.

Usilea allowed her gaze to drift around the room, taking in the many-paned glass windows and the carved wooden bookshelves nestled between them. Her older brother Jaric had personally overseen the building of this observatory as an early present for her coronation. A retreat for the queen of Edrin, recently turned eighteen. Her brother's regent period had ended, and she was ruling sovereign by their laws. It would be publicly celebrated at her coronation.

"I feel so old, and yet so young," she muttered. To whom? To the thick green leaves outside her window, rustling in the humid breeze. To the stars winking down at her through those leaves, faded stars that would soon be overcome by the new dawn. "I wonder when that will change?"

"*Perhaps when you begin to relax and enjoy your life.*" His dry voice filtered through her.

Quiet, you.

A soft awareness of laughter filled her mind. Usilea shook her head.

Heedless, his voice continued. "*Oh, the queen, here's the queen of sunlight, of starlight, arrayed in her tower of crystal dreams. Shall the queen of sunlight deign to visit the lord of nightmares? May it never be so.*"

His mocking humor, laced with sadness, cloaked her heart in a mist of unshed tears.

Usilea grimaced. *No nightmares have I seen in your dreams, my lord.*

"*And never shall you. For one such as you belongs to the daylight, to joy—even if you lurk in your tower like an all-seeing goldenbird.*"

A thread of longing wove around his words. Longing even his denial couldn't erase.

She sighed. *More riddles?*

"*My lips can never speak again ...*"

Usilea sat up in her chair, her pulse accelerating. He'd never said those words before. The plaintive honesty of them broke through her desire to continue the banter. *What do you mean?*

Only silence answered her for one minute.

Two.

Three.

"What do you mean?"

Only the ticking of the timepiece on the wall answered her. Only the sound of her own quick breaths filled the air.

"Answer me!" She stood, clutching her silken nightdress. "Please!"

"Lea?" Footsteps thudded up from behind the doorway. Usilea whirled around to face it. The next instant, a tall, broad-shouldered man yanked open the door. His forest-green eyes surveyed the room with a quick glance. "Are you all right?"

She breathed out slowly, a hand to her heart to calm it.

"Yes, Jaric. I am well."

"You were shouting." His low, blunt voice was laced with skepticism.

"Was I?" She wrapped composure around herself as easily as she pulled the layers of her robe tighter around her body. "Are you certain you didn't make a mistake?"

"I was nearby—and I heard you shouting."

Usilea raised her eyebrows as she stepped aside to allow him entrance. "Why were you nearby?"

A part of her knew, but she wanted to hear him say it, if only so her brother's voice could anchor her. Steady her after the abrupt disappearance of her friend.

A friend he could never know about. She had perhaps mentioned Petar once or twice as a child, but nothing since then. Her own comfort with her mild case of insanity was one matter, but she had enough to prove without giving her brother a reason to doubt. Jaric might even think it was a trace of their parents' influence, a trace of madness in her mind that could foment into something worse.

Their legacy already haunted her memories. They couldn't take her kingdom from her because of an unexplained malady.

He frowned. "I needed to … escape."

"Your beloved firstborns? Our country's precious heirs?"

Jaric's bronze forehead, a few shades lighter than her own deep brown skin though they were both tinged with garnet, wrinkled into deeper frown lines. "I love my daughter and my son. They are resting quietly under Renna's watch … in my study."

"Aha." Compassion stirred within her. Usilea stepped forward, placing her hands on his arms. "So you thought to find refuge in my observatory."

"Only for a few moments, and only if you were not using it," he shot back. "Then I heard you shouting."

"Oh, that was …" She trailed off, then her shoulders slouched and her cheeks heated. "Only a silly bit of nonsense within my head."

Certainly that was all it could be. Usilea fixed her eyes on her brother, at the warmth in his gaze and the gentler mood about him. Despite his desire for escape at this moment, married life and the work as a royal advisor suited him.

Jaric gave a grunt. "Your whimsical friend from when you were young? It can't be him again."

Stones. Why did her brother have such a good memory? But there was no deep worry in his aura, only light concern. Perhaps as a distraction from his own troubles.

"You know a woman of eighteen has no such flights of fancy." Did her voice tremble at the end? She tightened her jaw to still it.

"Good." His eyes narrowed, proof that he had caught the gesture. "The queen of Edrin must have a solid sense of her identity."

Usilea tightened her hold on his arms in warning. "I do. I promise you."

She simply had a friend who helped her with such matters. Perhaps it was childish, yet how could she expunge him from her mind? The very thought made her heart twist with horror.

"Very well." He pulled away from her and ran a hand through his wavy, dark brown hair. "I know you endured much from our parents. Remember, I am here for you." His voice turned gruff.

"And I you." He always had been, even when their parents tried to drive a wedge between them by making Usilea the crown princess. By inducting her in secret arts and knowledge at a young age and dismissing Jaric to the borderland skirmishes for weeks at a time, hoping to end the life of their son.

She stepped closer to him, allowing her unique ability to read and mimic Menders and other gifted individuals to seep out, to push aside his defenses. "You and Renna are the only family I have that I can rely on."

He snorted. "An easy statement to make, considering our parents are imprisoned for horrendous acts of violence against our people, and our relatives are trying to curry favors."

Usilea nodded. "Yes. But that doesn't diminish the truth of what I'm saying."

She reached out to touch his arm again, allowing the subtle mimicry to flow through her. To weave into his mind. Not compelling, only suggesting.

His shoulders relaxed a little. Then a little more.

"I know what you're doing," he said flatly. "Awareness negates the effects of mimicry."

"Of course it does." Usilea kept her voice warm and friendly. "You are most wise."

He turned to face her once more, smirking. "Flattery is not my favorite attire of yours, sister."

"Which means nothing, since I don't care about your opinion of my clothing." Usilea waved her hand around the room. "My space is yours. I was going to sleep soon, anyway."

"My thanks." He paused, then patted around his plain tunic and trousers. "Ah, I almost forgot. A message came for you from

Absteph. It arrived late tonight, but you are awake now. The courier said it was only to be opened by Queen Usilea Searlen herself."

"Indeed? Hmmm." She accepted the thick paper, tracing her fingers over the royal seal. The outline of a house with a flame within. Abstephians were known for their loyalty to home and family.

Her lips parted and dread squeezed her heart. Was this concerning her betrothal to Prince Cowan? Were they going to seek a formal wedding date at last? The marriage was to be consummated upon her eighteenth birthday, but the Abstephians had not reached out for a visit of state since she had become queen apparent. It had taken Usilea time to earn the trust over other countries whose leadership had been wary of her parents. She and Jaric had assumed Absteph was simply harder to win over due to their reserved reputation. Moreover, with the drought they had suffered over the last seasons, they might have more pride than usual—they had only reluctantly accepted Edrin's offer of assistance.

Carefully, Usilea pried open the seal, sensing the vague shadow nearby.

She repressed a smirk. Her friend could never resist peering at her mail.

Usilea read through the contents once, then again. The bottom fell out of her stomach. She reached for the comforting confines of her chair.

This was … unexpected.

"Lea? What is it?" Concern laced Jaric's tone.

"I am being invited to attend a royal funeral of state." Her voice faded. Usilea swallowed and breathed deeply. "My betrothed is dead. Along with most of the royal family of Absteph, including the crown prince."

She waited for a moment, expecting some commentary from

her inner friend. There was none. Perhaps he understood the gravity of the news as much as she did.

How could this be? There had been letters, albeit stilted and formal. There had been no news that Prince Cowan or the royal family had been in any danger.

Now, all were deceased due to some tragic illness, save for an uncle who would ascend the throne as the only remaining member of the bloodline.

How terrible.

How ... odd ...

Jaric broke through her thoughts. "Give me the letter."

She handed it over, accustomed to his abruptness when he was upset. Her brother scanned through the letter once, then twice. Then again. At last, he looked over at her.

"If you wish, I can attend in your stead."

"You are no longer my regent," Usilea said.

"I know. You must stay here to rule your kingdom. What if this is a trap so that they can entangle a Mender and keep you in Absteph?"

She huffed. "If it is, they will more easily keep a royal advisor than risk absconding with a queen."

"You have not been publicly crowned."

"According to our laws, that is a formality." Her parents had wanted to ensure her brother could never usurp her role, not that Jaric had any desire to do so. "And you have young children who need their father."

"You nearly die on sea travel."

"You exaggerate." But her guts roiled at the very idea of boarding a ship and crossing the channels to Absteph. While the country ran down the length of the coast east from Edrin, the capital city of

Hicareth was in the far north.

A shiver ran up her spine.

"There is something rotten about this." Her friend's voice was sharp and certain. *"You must go."*

I know. She let the words settle within her. Though she held little affection for the mysterious Prince Cowan, he and his family had perished unexpectedly. A grievous matter, and one that rang hollow within her.

In addition, this would be an opportunity to establish future relations with the country beyond the marriage alliance. She could bring over additional food stores as well. Usilea had grown used to proving herself. Now she had to do so again.

"I must go, Jaric. I *am* going as soon as a ship can be made ready."

Her brother glared at her for a moment. Usilea only raised her chin, staring back at him. Ultimately, she was his sovereign. It was her decision to make.

"…fine." His words were a growl. "I will see to your ship in the morning."

"Including food for them."

"Yes, their mysterious drought continues." She watched her brother stalk to a corner of the room and begin glancing through books. No doubt he would do his finest work to ensure her safety. It was better to leave him alone to his thoughts for now—and so she could continue thinking hers.

Usilea focused again on her mind as she walked through the doorway. *You do realize I'm going to be quite miserable on the voyage.*

"How shocking." His dry voice was even more arid. *"I will do my best to entertain you, goldenbird."*

You had better.

Between enduring sea travel and preparing for an unexpected appearance, she would take every ounce of distraction he could offer.

No matter if he did not, could not, could *never* exist, he was her friend.

Her dearest friend.

He would never leave her.

the midnight dew
falls through and through
the sunlit lands of me
of you
yet always remember
my darling true
there are thorns
at sunrise

you cannot say
my charming fellow
that the ground beneath
lies coarse and fallow
we will create
a new tomorrow
though there are thorns
at sunrise

he sidles by
beyond her reach
his mocking eyes
fringed with grief
she cannot escape
the cold belief
that they will part
when thorns come
at sunrise

CHAPTER TWO

He stood within a netherworld of shifting shadows and tortuous movements. The shapes moved. The shapes stilled. The shapes moved once more. Only ashen colors met his gaze in every direction.

Save for her. She of the golden eyes that glittered through the ashes, the narrow jaw that tilted just so when she was nervous, the midnight hair that was currently plaited in tiny braids away from her face.

Petar saw little else about her. He knew not the tone of her skin nor the arch of her brows nor the details of her figure. Yet in this miasmic nightmare, she alone was partially visible.

Golden eyes. Goldenbird.

Strong and fierce and gentle.

Currently, kneeling over a boxy-round shape in the corner of the room emptying her guts. From the weariness in her posture, he assumed it had happened once already. Twice a day was typical for her sailing voyages.

He sat next to her, wishing he could hold her or comfort her in some way. If she so desired it. She was quite changeable in her own quiet way, sometimes preferring company, often preferring silence and solitude.

An endless mystery herself.

Instead, he hummed a soft tune to her, one he remembered from childhood. Whenever that had been. At times, Petar knew things. He was the youngest of his family. They had been amazed at him and frightened for him. He had been raised in a mysterious wood. He could move … he could fashion …

The tendrils slipped away from him once more, as they always did. The same way her name escaped his memory, and he never seemed to speak his name in a way she could retain. More puzzles. More riddles.

Riddles were his only family.

Lord of nightmares that I carry alone.

After another moment, she lifted her head from the receptacle and turned to him. Her golden eyes were even more weary than before, though there was a calm in their depths. The result of his simple ditty? Perhaps.

"I almost regret the journey." She stood. The wavering edges of her figure conveyed her to a nearby larger boxy edifice. A desk of some kind. Petar's memories of his life might be subdued like thornflowers at sunset, but he could name objects and other facts.

He followed her in that nebulous way that movement occurred here. More of hovering than exact steps. It didn't matter how. He was by her side.

Have your Mender relatives or your physicians still not mastered a potion for your sea ailment? Petar tried and failed to keep the frustration from his voice.

The area where her lips should be moved in a way that indicated a frown, as much as he could detect from the shadows. *"They do what they can. There are not cures for every condition."*

For yours, there should be.

Those golden eyes rolled up to the ceiling within her enshad-owed face. *"Sometimes, one must just suffer. And I will."* She paused. *"It is quite awful, though."*

Naturally, it is. He moved to stare over her shoulder at the pages laid out over the desk. The words came into sharp focus, unaffected by the fog that otherwise distorted his vision. The sight reminded him of what he had been doing before … disappearing. *I have made some study of the history and customs of Absteph.*

He hardly needed to. Petar knew that country as well as he knew himself, for some odd reason. No, he knew the country better than himself, for he barely recalled key details of his life. Or when he would next wake, and why he only woke around her. The lovely, intelligent queen.

She nodded. *"Have you discovered anything of note regarding the royal family?"*

No. They live, they grow, they wed, they pass on. Some of these histories are lies.

"How can you know that, clever boy?"

She teased him again, poked fun at his tendency to make flippant judgements. Though these words were not flippant. Even if he didn't know the origin of his words, they were true.

Abstephians guard their family above all else. They value strong homes, strong families, and strong character. Still, they are also mortal beings, and what one values, one will bend rules to attain. If he had lips, they would be smiling thinly. *There are thorns at sunrise.*

"Yes, so you often say."

An Abstephian phrase, apparently. It means to beware appearances and times of ease, for hardship and deceit will come as surely as life itself.

The phrase was a warning as well, though he could not remember why.

Her sadness flowed through him. "*I know difficulty and deceit well.*"

You have known it too much. Then, because Petar knew she would be irritated at any hint of a patronizing tone, he continued. *But you have come through all the stronger, silver queen, goldenbird.*

A shy warmth replaced her sadness. Even now, she knew not how precious she was—or she often forgot. The result of focusing on those around her rather than on herself.

He would always remind her.

"*The gift of Absteph is intriguing.*" She turned over another paper. "*Makers. All people bear some measure of it and use it in daily life for the benefit of their family and community. So I, as a Mender queen, will not be unusual to them. Moreover, I have an advantage because I should be able to read their auras. I was able to do so with the visiting emissaries, the Stormers and Warpers and Hunters.*"

So you were.

"*Manipulating emotions will be off the table, though. Others with Gifts sense it far too easily.*"

It would also not be sporting.

"*Hmmm, yes. Astonishing how my parents tried to erase all knowledge of other types of gifts from our people. Such a horrible desire to control.*" She scanned a fresh page. "*Makers can shape specific materials with their hands alone. The type of material one can shape is often passed down in families. More powerful Makers can shape multiple kinds of materials. The most powerful are rumored to Make creations with their minds alone.*"

Hmmm. Her words rippled the memories within him, revealing … pain. Searing pain from his forehead, from his fingers, as they drew from him again and again. Petar would not fail them. He would give all he had and then, perhaps, the agony would cease.

As quickly as it emerged, the pain vanished. Only a string of words remained. *Make it once, make it twice, make it from amber, make it from ice.*

"You and your rhymes." Her lips moved. This time, he could barely see the outline of a smile. Not enough. Petar wanted, craved to see her smile. Yet if an outline was all he would ever see, he would rather remain unsatisfied than never know her at all.

The goldenbird returned to her pages. *"Makers are common among the populace. Indeed, it is unheard of for someone to not possess a portion of the gift. The individual Making gift is strongest in one's home area ..."*

As her mental voice trailed off into deep, focused reading, Petar's attention was drawn to the reason they were traveling to this funeral rather than sending her brother. The strange, certain intuition they had both shared.

Something was amiss. All but one of the royal family, suddenly dead? This uncle suddenly in charge as the only remaining heir of the lineage? Were it any other country, he would suspect foul play, but an Abstephian would never betray their family line in such a way. It was abhorrent, anathema to everything that he—no, they—believed.

Although, as he listened to the pattering rhythms of Usilea's mind, the beats of her quicker-than-quick reading, he was relieved about one aspect of this situation.

Her betrothed had perished. She was bound to no man.

What of the alliance with Absteph, queen of starlight?

Her head looked up from the parchment. *"I suppose I must broker another sort. I can do it. There must be a way. The partnership between our countries has been beneficial and must continue."*

Indeed.

"A pity I may not marry you, my imaginary friend." Her voice turned light and whimsical once more. *"You already know my secrets, and I yours. We are used to each other's faults and work with them. For you are from my mind."*

I am nothing of the sort. He did all he could to project a huff. *If I am of your creation, why can you never guess the answers to my riddles?*

"My mind hides knowledge from itself."

As does mine. That is little excuse.

Her words struck truer than she knew, albeit in a different manner. She could not marry him. He was no one, whatever he was. He could not see his own hand, much less trace the delicate outline of her insubstantial face.

A face that abruptly crumpled into a shadowy mess. She jolted to her feet and ran for the corner of the room.

He followed close behind, his heart pinching with sympathy and revulsion.

Hopefully they would reach the shores of Absteph soon.

could you find me
if you might
if you may
seek me out
in endless days
the twisting maze
if you find me
in the ways
you might escape
the frightful maze

I will find you
if I might
if I may
I will seek you out
in endless days
the twisting maze
I will find you
in the ways
we will escape
the frightful maze

for I will never
live without you

you may have to
live without me

never, no never
will I live
without …

CHAPTER THREE

Shimmering charcoal waters lapped at the rocky shoreline in the twilight of early evening. The waves broadened into a deep harbor, where Her Majesty's ship *The Seaspoken* was docked. Safely on shore, Usilea could admit that the prow of the vessel was magnificent, that the swoop of the planking was elegant, and that the sight of *The Seaspoken* against the distant, fiery mountains of Absteph was truly awe-inspiring.

I dread the morning I must ascend into the depths of the beast once more.

Her friend's grim humor flickered through her. "*I as well. So much of your world is sheathed in shadows to me, so why are certain foul excretions so visible?*"

A mystery to us both. Why don't you solve it, clever boy? She turned away from the ship to face the dock ahead of her, her fingers running along the golden embroidery of the heavy, dark blue cloak she wore over her finest traveling dress. She had made visits of state before, but never for the funeral of the man she was meant to marry.

"*I would sooner scrub a dragon's rear.*"

There have been dragons in Absteph, or so it is rumored. You might have an opportunity. Usilea blinked innocently. How silly of her. As though he could truly see her. As though he were real.

"You have royal guards in plenty. Sentence a squadron of them to this task."

The poor guards. Whatever did they do? A grin escaped her as she took in the four guards that surrounded her.

Then her gaze expanded to take in the landscape of Absteph itself. The stone harbor was nestled in a small village on a plain of grayish-green grass, as though life was desperately trying to emerge amidst the drought. How odd, considering the ground itself looked soaked through, and tiny flowers and yellow stalks pockmarked the gently sloping hill beyond the village. Was it something within the soil itself? A lack of some essential mineral?

At that moment, a party of officials in the black and silver of Absteph strode toward them. Her spine stiffened. She quickly assumed a pleasant, somber attitude more appropriate for a time of mourning.

"You are wise and capable." With those words, she sensed her imaginary friend drift away, the faint echoes of vague shadows dissipating around her. Over the course of twelve years, he had learned when she needed to focus.

If only he were alive. She could think of no one better to stand at her side.

Usilea pushed the foolish thought aside, turning her attention to the gentleman before her. The letter had included a small drawing of Reign Lord Aeson Gunnarthin, as he was known in the interim before his confirmation and coronation as the monarch of Absteph. However, the spare sketch had not included the strong lines of his jaw, the crispness of his short, silvery hair, or the lightness of his blue eyes. And they certainly hadn't included his height, over a foot taller than her.

She inhaled and exhaled imperceptibly. She was below average height for a woman of Edrin, so it was not difficult to find others who were taller than her. It was also not difficult to find the condescending demeanor.

"Queen Usilea Searlen." His voice was as silky as the silver robes he wore. "You honor us with your presence."

"Thank you, Reign Lord Gunnarthin. I only wish the reason had been happier."

He held his hands out, palms flat and facing up. She did likewise, allowing her fingertips to barely touch his. The Reign Lord's skin stained faintly greenish-red.

"Call me Lord Aeson, Your Majesty. We were at one time to be family." His hands remained extended.

She hid a frown. His skin tones suggested some mixture of irritation and … jealousy? Envy? Abstephian skin tone variations were hard to discern, particularly with only basic study. However, his aura was decidedly peeved. *What does he expect?*

"He wants you to place your hands on his, palms down, so that he might clasp yours and raise the backs of your hands to his cheeks." Her friend's words were dismissive and annoyed.

That would be flirting. He's twenty years my senior. Moreover, she could read his aura, which meant that with physical contact she would also be able to sense any injuries and heal them. This was not the time to Receive.

"He has never met a woman he would not attempt to beguile."

Usilea paused. *How do you know that?*

"… I don't know." The voice retreated once more in her mind.

She returned to the present. Usilea knew that an extended,

controlled pause showed that she would not be pushed into any action. At least, so her parents had taught her. Though they were horrifically misguided in many areas, they did know something of leadership.

"Very well, Lord Aeson." She withdrew her hands, granting him one request while denying another. "Thank you for meeting me here."

"The pleasure is all mine." One of his hands retreated within his cloak, then emerged once more. A small piece of wood rested in his palm. "A token of Absteph."

The wood lifted in the air as though by a string, then whirled around in his hand. Parts carved off it of their own accord. Wonder overcame her irritation as he used his gift of Making to turn the wood into an intricate sculpture. In a few moments, an image of her ship, *The Seaspoken*, floated down to rest in his palm once more. The sails, prow, and all other parts were realized with breathtaking detail.

"For you, Your Majesty."

"Thank you, Lord Aeson." She nodded to one of her guards to accept the token, then gave the Abstephian a bright smile. "What a thrilling display."

"Now you have a smaller version of the ship to haunt your dreams."

Quiet. She fought the urge to roll her eyes. "We have brought additional shipments of food."

"Your altruism is commendable."

"Thank you." Did he need more of a nudge? "I look forward to seeing your capital city, Reign Lord."

"So you shall. Right this way to Hicareth."

They fell into step, as much as the protection of their guards would allow. Usilea turned her face into the cool breeze. Hicareth was in the northernmost reaches of Absteph, which made it far colder than her own capital city Syrus, located in the southern region of Edrin.

Lord Aeson maintained a steady stream of conversation while they ascended the narrow pavement up the side of the harbor to a small carriage. She learned about how the citizens relied on underground aquifers of steaming water to heat their homes. How most of the gray-and-white stone buildings were only one story to allow for greater fortification against earthquakes. That the wild springs of hot water were considered to have great medicinal properties.

All things she had learned on the voyage over, yet she didn't bother interrupting him. He seemed to enjoy talking, and it gave her more time to observe. Most of the people they passed on the street wore tan-colored clothing and had bluish-brown tinged skin. Both the clothing and the skin tones were signs that they were grieving. In contrast, neither Lord Aeson nor his guards were garbed in tan, nor did their auras portray grief.

Perhaps they had greater control over their feelings than most?

The misgivings within her rose once more. Something was wrong.

Who am I to think with such suspicion? I have only just arrived to this country. A man can be inappropriately flirtatious without being a villain. I could be reading his aura wrong.

None of the thoughts silenced her uneasiness.

Where is your wisdom, clever boy?

Silence.

She nudged harder in her mind. A strange buzzing filled her mind, then a sense of startlement. *Are you daydreaming?*

"*Nightmaring, I suppose. Have you noticed how shoddy the people look?*"

I assumed they were mourning.

"*That does not excuse the thinness of their faces or raggedness of their* clothing." His voice was grim. "*Something is amiss. We are a small people. There should be enough resources for all.*"

You knew of the drought. Also, what do you mean, 'we?' Are you of Absteph, now?

No answer. Usilea's lips twitched downward. She smoothed her expression into complacency once more. Composure was a key asset in letting others underestimate her. They often read it as insecurity.

"You seem very knowledgeable in the ways of your kindred," she said, giving Lord Aeson a demure smile.

He straightened on the seat, adjusting his robes. "All the better to serve them, Your Majesty." Faint red-orange touched the edges of his face, emphasized by his aura. He had received her flattery well—and wanted her to know it. "If you would direct your gaze to the right, you can see the Willowing Halls."

She did as he said. In truth, the palace of Hicareth was … a touch underwhelming. At least compared to Menirose Palace of Syrus. That palace, her home for the last eighteen years, was brightly colored in shades of yellow and blue and red, with turrets soaring to the sky and elaborate gardens.

In contrast, the Willowing Halls was a modest, albeit curious, structure. A broad, one-story base, made of gray-and-white stone with small windows cut out at various points, and then a second story, half as big as the first, positioned equidistantly atop it. Out of the center of the structure rose a long, narrow spire of silvery-white rock reaching up to the skies.

"Interesting," she muttered. Then, louder, "Did you build your palace around the spire, then?"

"Our ancestors did, many centuries ago. The Skyspear is said to have properties that deflect any eruptions from the Decla Mountains in the north." He studied the edifice with great satisfaction.

The carriage wheels rattled closer to the palace. "I thought, given Edrin's own connection in precious stones, you would understand our reliance on our land. Though our connection does not extend to skin shades."

His gaze lingered over her. Usilea resisted the urge to recoil at this ogling of her garnet-touched, deep brown skin, although she did allow her eyes to dip down in seeming modesty. The people of Edrin had mineral-touched skin, the type of which depended on where they had been born. The truth was that simple, and she was accustomed to some fascination from others, but his leer was disturbing. "A ... unique perception, Lord Aeson."

"Thank you, Your Majesty." He gave her a final, lingering glance.

An unpleasant chill crept down her spine, one that had nothing to do with the brisk weather outside the carriage. She couldn't escape these confines soon enough.

"He oversteps." Her friend's voice echoed with anger in her mind. *"As though you are a peculiarity to be approved of and collected."*

Perhaps others have viewed Abstephians the same way, with their changing skin tones.

"At times. We seldom travel. And Abstephians are reserved about such matters when outside the family. Feelings revealed by skin tone is knowledge that is not spoken about. We note the shifting colors only with the most delicate phrases."

Again, you say 'we,' my friend.

"So I do."

She waited for additional words, but as before, he gave none. Perhaps she had learned so much about Absteph that a part of her identified with the people? The idea was thin, but Usilea was distracted by the fury building within her toward Lord Aeson. She was young, yes, but that did not make her some ingenue to be toyed with or patronized.

Thank the Eternal, at that moment the carriage came to a stop near the back of the palace. A broad green lawn stretched out before her eyes, interrupted by a polished black stone path running down the middle. To one side of the path was a large square bordered by three-foot-tall urns filled with silver-white flowers with thick circles of petals. Here, at least, the drought had not touched the land.

"They are thornflowers." Her imaginary friend spoke quietly, almost reverently. *"They symbolize the fragility of life and death, ease and difficulty. The stems are smooth at night, then the thorns and blossoms emerge at sunrise. Those thorns are tipped with poison that paralyzes the surrounding skin if pricked."*

Paralyzes?

He seemed to chuckle. *"Only for a few moments. These blossoms are tamed for public use. Their poison deters foolish zarbucks, not beings like us. One would receive far more poison from wild thornflowers."*

Usilea exited the carriage behind Lord Aeson. "The flowers are lovely."

"Traditional thornflowers." He bowed his head briefly. "They are considered sacred to our people, particularly the royal family. Enjoy them with your lovely eyes, but do not touch."

Hm. He is less than forthcoming.

"Why would he reveal when he can conceal?" Her friend's bitterness was tangible. *"It is the Abstephian way, at least for him."*

"The funeral begins in one hour. Regrettably, duties call me elsewhere." The Reign Lord gave her another approving look-over. "Palace guards will escort you in my stead." He focused on her face intently, his voice softening. "I cannot begin to convey how much your attendance gladdens my heart, Your Majesty. In the midst of grief, your freshness offers hope for new alliances ahead."

He extended his hands in the customary gesture that they had exchanged upon her arrival—for that gesture was also a leave-taking. As before, she gave the polite response instead of offering her hands for him to clasp. Did disappointment show in his eyes? It certainly did in his aura, and greenish-red seeped into the edges of his skin.

"Absteph's hospitality is a welcome respite, Lord Aeson. I will see you at the funeral."

As soon as she turned away from him, Usilea grimaced. Her hands briefly clenched her cloak. Of all the stone-cursed impertinence! Her freshness and new alliances? He might as well have offered her a marriage proposal at that moment.

Would he? The light gray walls were a blur around her as she and her contingent of guards followed the palace guards to her suite. After the funeral, he could offer his hand, citing the value of making the bond between their countries even though her betrothed was dead.

Quick, snapping steps led her inside the simple room, dominated by a bed carved of polished dark wood and a chest of drawers of the same wood. Rods of silver rose out of the wood, suspending a mirror between them. Flames leaped in a large stone fireplace with a mantle featuring molded thornflower vines.

Once her guards had inspected the room and the adjoining relieving space for threats, Usilea bade them to wait outside for a few moments. To collect her thoughts, she said.

As soon as the door shut, she strode over to the absurdly large bed and collapsed across it on her back. Her cloak muddled with her movements, covering her face. She let it be. Let the fabric hide her for a handful of sweet, quiet moments. Away from the expectations, the pageantry, the intrigue.

There was only her and the blankness behind her eyes as she fell into a doze.

Only a few, brief moments to enjoy rest on the stable ground instead of the ceaseless rocking of the ship. It always required a sleeping tonic.

"You will have to face them eventually."

She sighed. *Then allow me my solitude.*

"Thirty minutes have already passed."

"What?" The words came out as a gasp. She flung the cloak off her face and sat up. "Why didn't you warn me?"

A knocking sounded at the door. "Your Majesty? Are you well?"

"Yes! Yes, I am." She pressed a hand over her heart, glaring at the nothingness of vague shadows and stretched air.

"You needed to rest. There is time for you to prepare. It is ill manners to arrive early at an Abstephian funeral. It implies that you are anticipating the grief."

Usilea shook her head. *I don't remember you having so much knowledge of Absteph in all our years together.*

"I suppose … I am Abstephian."

Surprise filtered through her. *You are? You didn't mention that.*

This lent the idea of her identifying with the local people more credence, did it not? Perhaps?

She summoned Rilva, who also functioned as her lady-in-waiting. The guard quickly set about arranging her hair and assisting her into fresh clothes. They were layers of soft tan, in keeping with Abstephian mourning garb.

"… I wasn't permitted … perhaps."

He wasn't permitted? What did that mean? How would an imaginary friend not be permitted to say something? Was it some barrier in her mind?

"Your Majesty, we are finished." Rilva stepped back with a half-bow.

Usilea could give his words no further thought. All of her mind focused on the ceremony before her.

She reached the funeral procession at the precise time it was beginning. Others assembled into the line just as swiftly and seemingly at last minute. Everyone wore soft garments in shades of tan similar to hers, fastened with simple belts or buttons. The soft yellow-cream shades of approval that tinted the Abstephians around her indicated she had done well by choosing to honor their custom and clothing. Usilea's heart beat with the flickering torchlight as she settled into her cloak.

Then the procession began. She recalled what else she knew of Abstephian funerals. The attendees wove in two lines around the five platforms that held each of the five bodies. Then at specific times, they paused while the local priest of the Eternal intoned a soft prayer. The ceremony would end when each part of the line had paused in front of each platform. Usilea had only to follow the individual in front of her, a tall young woman with a cap of chin-length dark hair.

As she neared the first platform, the unrest from earlier slithered into her stomach. That sense of something askew, of something *wrong*, prodded at her mind. Her fingers twitched. Usilea clasped her hands together. There was nothing amiss.

Everything was amiss. Every piece of the puzzle absent, every bone and muscle out of joint.

Her line paused so that she stood in front of the first platform. The one that held Prince Cowan. Her betrothed. He was clad in a more traditional Abstephian tunic and robe in deep reds, blues, and charcoals.

Something within her wrenched as she looked down at him. At his stark white hair and skin. All Abstephians naturally bleached white upon death.

The sight of him struck an ominous, clanging knell within her.

This isn't him. It looked like the paintings she had been sent, enough to fool others. But this wasn't … it couldn't be … something was—

"You are right, goldenbird. That is not Prince Cowan. That is an imposter."

How do you know?

"Because … I think … I know …" His words drifted off, and something seemed to ripple from out of the corner of her eye.

"Because I'm the prince." The dry voice, crackling with warmth, intoned from a figure standing across from her on the other side of the platform. "Wait, how can that be true? But it is. I know it is."

Mismatched eyes, one the color of sapphire and the other rose quartz, stared down at the body on the pedestal, then turned to face her. His white-blond hair fell past his shoulders, long and tangled. Dirt smudged his wide, elegant face which narrowed to a strong, angular jaw. His skin was tinged with reds and browns. He was upset and frustrated.

He was hers.

Her mouth fell open. Somehow, beyond all doubt, she knew this man.

Before her stood her imaginary friend.

In the flesh.

CHAPTER FOUR

He could see her.

After unknowable years of listening to her, speaking with her, arguing with her, standing with her in the shadows—Petar could truly see her.

She was beautiful.

Her golden eyes widened as she stared back at him, eyes framed by elegantly shaped black brows set against rich brown skin tinged with deep garnet. Nostrils flared in a strong, perfect nose, and her firm, dark red lips were twisted in a grimace. The next second, her gentle face was similarly contorted.

Why was she glaring at him? Scared of him?

Skies above, could she *see* him?

"How is this—what are you doing here?" Her words were a fierce whisper, causing the young woman in front of her to glance back curiously.

Her face flushed a rosier garnet tint as she was nudged along in her ceremonial line. He followed suit, walking along with her. Her gaze followed him.

He remembered her name. Usilea. A beautiful name for a magnificent woman who existed. Indeed, why wouldn't she exist? Were all of their years of friendship meaningless?

No. Never.

She had always existed.

"You can see me!" He glanced around them. None had stirred at his words. "But no one else can, can they?"

What a strange marvel. Petar looked down at himself. There he stood, in black trousers and a black tunic, both ripped and slashed in parts but serviceable. His hands were veined with dirt as though he had been clawing through the earth. Toward what end, he didn't remember. White strands of hair reached his upper chest.

When had his hair grown that long? The last thing he remembered … was nothing. A blank was there. But he knew he was the prince. Of that, he was certain.

Usilea's expression had smoothed into her usual placidity. Her eyes gleamed. "*How is this possible?*"

"How could it not be, goldenbird?" She was moving again in the ceremonial line. Petar sped along with her. "We have been speaking through extraordinary, mysterious means for so long. Now there is slightly less mystery." He scrubbed a hand at his disheveled clothing. "Although you appear to be far more prepared for this meeting than I am."

She wore the same shades of tan as his people. The Abstephian people.

"*I doubt anyone expected you to be here. Even you, apparently.*" She was flustered beneath the hard-fought veneer of calm.

Naturally, she was flustered. She was in an unfamiliar place trying to go along with an unfamiliar ritual and her trusted friend had appeared out of nowhere before her. Her composure was impressive.

Frostmelt! She had moved ahead of him once more. He strode toward her part of the line, noting absently that the young woman in front of Usilea seemed to be following him with her gaze as well. Though she didn't seem to focus on him specifically, more of the area around him.

"Usilea, I'm sorry for the disturbance, but you must be aware that I have no control over this manifestation. We need to—"

"*Shhh. He's speaking.*"

Ah yes, the priest of the Eternal was intoning the traditional passing-on words. Petar studied the platform before him. It was meant to be the one for the former king of Absteph, King Andryn.

His shoulders knotted. Whoever the individual was, he was not his father, the true king. Something was wrong in the angle of his jaw, in the carving of his features. He was merely a clever facsimile. Who would exact such a deception?

Lord Aeson would. The thought dropped through him like an icicle falling from a tall building. The Reign Lord was capable of many things both gruesome and treacherous.

An image surfaced in his mind of the silver-haired man scowling at him across a clearing of warped, rotten plants and half-burned walls. *They are weak and, in the end, so are you.*

As soon as the priest stopped speaking, Petar began again. "This is a farce. Every single one of these people are imposters."

Tragic imposters, for they were dead, but false nonetheless.

"*How can they be?*"

"There are some among Absteph who can shape skin with their hands."

Her nose twitched with repugnance. "*While they are still alive?*"

"It is forbidden, but yes. After death, certainly."

"*What proof do you have?*"

Petar exhaled in frustration. "I don't know! I've only recently come to myself. Something about this place, this land …"

It was awakening him, reminding him. Or maybe it was Usilea's presence there, her deep, compelling self that drew him to her, calling him more to himself. Though he had spoken with her in earlier years when he had known more. *Had* he known more?

Sharp pain sliced through his skull. He pressed a hand to his forehead, trying to massage the muscles there—if they were truly there at all. How was any of this occurring?

"*What's wrong? … Cowan? You are Cowan?*"

"The pain is fading now." He glanced over at her. "Petar, please. Cowan is … less familiar to me."

They hadn't told him. For so long, they had kept it and him a secret.

"*Petar. Why does that seem—*" She stopped again—or tried to. This time, the woman in front of her grabbed her arm and tugged her forward. Petar fell into step once again.

"Come with me," the woman said quietly, her cadence quick with abrupt variations and clipped endings. "Act as though you are faint."

"What?" Usilea tried to discreetly pull her arm away. "I am no such thing."

"No, but you are distracted by a strange warping of the air across from you." The woman paused while the priest spoke aloud, then continued. "Abstephians are superstitious about fainting at a funeral procession. They believe it a sign of deeply empathizing with the dead, a sign of honoring them. You'll save face more than all your sudden pauses."

Usilea frowned at her.

"She's right," Petar added quickly. "It's a good idea. I will be right with you."

"*Yes. You will.*" Her words were soft iron.

The next second, she sank down, a hand fluttering over her chest. The strange woman caught her and steadied her, resting the queen's head against her shoulder. Petar rushed ahead as well—then stopped short of the platform. The dead were false in appearance, but he would not dishonor them by walking through them in even a phantasmal way. Instead, he quickly darted around and through the line.

At this point, the young woman was guiding the queen across the lawn, ignoring the black stone pathway. With a few quick words to the guards at the palace entrance, they entered the light gray corridors. Usilea began to straighten from her half-swoon.

"Not yet, Your Majesty. Let's keep the ruse a bit longer." The tall woman stopped in front of a particular door, nodded to the guards on either end, then stepped inside. Petar had to rush to avoid being left behind. As it was, the door pushed through part of his heels, sending a strange ache through him. A sort of phantom pain.

"Who are you?" Usilea demanded, slightly breathless. Her fingers clutched something inside her cloak—a tiny dagger. Smart woman.

The woman turned around, hands on her hips. "Lady Li-Ann Kwen Throgmorton of Nyark."

Nyark. A land to the west, beyond Edrin and the Otlan Sea. It would explain the accent and the gears and bits of metal adorning her hair, skin, and clothing. But Kwen was a Sukeish name, which would align with her appearance.

She spoke more. "Just call me Larkin. And you are Queen Usilea Searlen of Edrin, who is in some way speaking with a warp disturbance. How is that?"

"Warp disturbance?" The queen's brow wrinkled. "I am doing no such thing. I'm merely conversing with … my friend."

Petar nodded. "Good answer."

"Are there dead Warpers in Edrin, then?"

"Excuse me?" Usilea blinked.

"Warpers. People gifted with the ability to bend and shape the essence of the realms. When we fail to Warp properly or fall ill, we can be consumed by the essence and turn into ghosts. Warp disturbances." She scuffed a hand through her hair, unsettling the gear-like fastenings. "Although they aren't common."

With a look of infinite patience, Usilea answered, "No, there are no Warpers within Edrin that I'm aware of. Though you go where you will, regardless."

"We have our own rules about travel. When I follow them."

"Why are you here at all?" Petar demanded. "Why help us?"

Usilea relayed his words to Larkin.

"I'm here as a noble trade liaison. Abstephians like tea and other exotic goods, and Warper houses are uniquely good at providing them. As for why I helped you," she shrugged, "I grew tired of the funeral. I've attended too many lately, and while noble guests are expected to go to ceremonies like that, they don't have to stay for the whole time. I saw an escape, and I took it. Besides, I'm a curious sort."

"You don't speak like a noblewoman," Usilea replied. Indeed, Larkin seemed to float in and out of more polished speech at her whim.

"I can, when I want or have to." Larkin's dark brown eyes focused on the area where Petar stood—well, nearly the area. Her gaze was out of focus. Small gears on either edge of her eyebrows glinted, seemingly of their own light. "You say your friend isn't a dead Warper, but he's somehow rippling in and out of our tangible realm. How is this so?"

Usilea raised her eyebrows, affecting innocence. "I do not know. I'm afraid I can be of little assistance to you, Lady Throgmorton—"

"Larkin. Please." She pursed her lips and tapped her bronze-plated nails on her reticule. "I'm not stupid, Your Majesty."

Petar winced. That was the wrong tactic.

"I am not someone to be interrupted, Lady Throgmorton." That same soft iron threaded Usilea's voice. "The crown of Edrin is grateful for your assistance, but I must be on my way—"

"He'll disappear if you don't do something soon. Your friend, that is." Larkin didn't wave or move aside. "From the way you keep looking at the spot, I assume it's a he. An attractive one, at that." She glanced at a bronze-and-leather band on her wrist with tiny spin-ning dials, then frowned. "But with the instability in the warping, he won't last."

Fear crawled up his spine. "Does she speak the truth?"

"How should I know?" Usilea's jaw worked as she turned back to the woman from Nyark. As with other Warpers, her aura was fuzzy around the edges, though she did seem sincere. "How can you say this? Do you know what happened to him?"

"Not a bit. But I can read the ripples. Has he shown any signs of pain since he popped up?"

Petar and Usilea nodded at the same time.

"Then whatever was done to him is taking a toll, somehow. He has five days, at the most, if the degradation doesn't happen too fast." Larkin pulled a small, round object out of a pocket of her long tan skirt and took a bite. Some kind of fruit? He couldn't smell it to be certain. "You need to deal with this soon."

Otherwise the last of the true rulers would fall with Petar. This, he knew.

Usilea drew her hands into her sleeves, a habit formed out of trying to conceal hand wringing when she was a child. He knew because he had been there, telling her stories or jokes to keep her from the worried gesture. Now, Petar reached out as though to take her hands.

"What are you doing?" She eyed him curiously.

"Trying to … offer comfort …"

"Oh?"

"It was a foolish idea." He forced a smile. "My fingers would likely pass through yours. Usilea, the time is so short, and you are not equipped to find me."

She paused, her face softening. *"Do you think I would leave you to fade away?"*

"You thought me imaginary. Imaginary things fade, don't they?" He couldn't blame her thoughts, yet the memory of them stung.

"You are my closest friend and now you are here, standing before me. As Prince Cowan … Petar … my betrothed. I cannot ignore that." Usilea's hands moved within her robe where she was almost certainly wringing them. *"I would never ignore that."*

The quiet sadness like evening rain melted the bitterness threatening his heart. Matters had changed rapidly. All they could do was adapt to them. "I believe you."

"Good." Her shoulders relaxed a fraction as she stepped closer to him. *"Now, you said those on the platforms were imposters, and you remembered that you were the prince. How do you know this?"*

Petar's mind spun as he tried to put the formless into words. He knew the same way he knew Usilea would always be there, even through his bitterness. The way he knew every twist and turn of this palace, every small crevice wherein to play hide-and-seek. The way he knew the deception in Reign Lord Aeson's manner.

"I belonged here. Even though I did not know in what manner at first."

With that knowing came fresh agony arcing through his skull and his side. He groaned, seizing his head with both hands.

"Petar?" Usilea's voice pitched higher with fear. *"What is it?"*

He gritted his teeth. "It is …"

After a moment, the pain faded, leaving him weak-kneed. He had enough pride left for that. When he was able to focus on the queen, she was much closer, staring up at him with concern.

"It is … this place. He takes from it. He takes from me."

"What do you mean?"

"Lord of nightmares, lord of dreams untold. Lord of pain and sorrow for the sake of those I love. There are thorns at sunrise."

"Petar!"

He cracked a smile. "I don't remember."

Usilea's expression gentled. *"I'm trying to understand. You always mentioned living in the wilds of a mysterious wood. How are you a prince?"*

"Do you think I lie?"

"No. But I'm confused."

Petar shook his head. "As was I. I was told … when I was older. Before then, I believed myself only a foundling, raised by royal guardians of the wood. I would visit the palace, and I remember playing with the royal family but never for too long. In Absteph, the barriers between sovereign and subject are less rigid than in Edrin."

"Why not tell me, then?"

"I … forgot." He winced against another onslaught of pain. "What was known so recently slipped out so suddenly. It was all … I could do … to find you. Somehow."

"Now, I will find you." Her face sobered as she considered his words and the meaning behind them. She was a queen, after all. She was always a queen.

One certainty filtered through him. While he had been angry at being raised in secret and being lied to about his parentage, he had also felt relieved. He could marry the woman he loved, for they had been betrothed this entire time. The joy of that revelation had equaled the anger at the deception.

Then, the monster had attacked and …

A throat cleared. Larkin. "So, have you and your friend decided on a course of action?"

"I must discover what happened to the royal family," he said.

"We need to stop Petar from fading," Usilea stated instead. "How would we do that?"

He scowled at her. "Usilea, you are not able—"

"You need to find where his body is located," Larkin answered. "Whatever you are seeing is not the full shape and form of him. If you can find where he actually is, then body can unite with spirit once more."

"Usilea—"

"So it will be."

How could someone so mild sound so authoritative? He admired it, yet now, he also found it infuriating. "I will not have you die in search of me."

"Then I will not die." She reached for his hand, her own slipping through it with a faint ache. *"You are worth finding first. Then we will discover the truth of the imposters. I promise."*

He opened his mouth to argue further, to insist she try to learn the truth about the others. His family, though he hadn't known them as such for most of his life.

Her stubborn look would not be denied. Beneath were deeper, softer feelings that tugged at his heart, promising things she might be unaware of but things he dared hope were promises of their future to come.

At last, Petar nodded. "Very well."

"But how shall we do this? A queen cannot simply abandon her hosts for a quest."

Aha, a problem. Safer territory.

He smiled slowly. "I think I know of a way."

Another shock of pain ricocheted through him, obscuring all thought. Before he could speak, Usilea, Larkin, and the room vanished.

do not dare
to leave me here
apart from the brilliance
of your smile

are you sure
you want me here
awash with the chaos
of my soul

I am no
stranger to you
awash in the chaos
of your soul

you may yet
regret your words

I will never
regret my words

I only regret
you leaving me
to say them
alone

CHAPTER FIVE

He hadn't returned. No voice speaking, not a twisting of ridiculous words that made her smile even while they perplexed her. Not even a nonsensical ditty that hinted at wonders beyond her imagining.

Nothing, save for the bits of haunting verse that fitful sleep had permitted her to remember upon waking.

When she woke, tears leaked out of her eyes and dropped onto the silken fabric of her pillow. For the absence of him. For worry of what had happened. For fear that she might never see him again.

"Petar," she whispered quietly enough so that the two guards wouldn't hear. In her home of Menirose Palace, they remained outside her chamber, for there were guards stationed everywhere. Here in Willowing Halls, they remained nearby at all times, save when she specifically requested solitude. Usilea respected the need for security. Rilva and Pelreira had proven their loyalty time and again over the years.

Yet at this moment, she only wished to be alone with her thoughts, except if she be interrupted by her imaginary friend's—by her *friend's* presence.

"Petar." The words were so strange coming out of her lips. He had a name. He was from Absteph. He was her betrothed, had been her betrothed this entire time.

A twinge of hideous doubt tugged at her. Was this all a ruse? A trick of her own mind? Or maybe he was someone else who had made a mistake.

No. It could not be so.

Petar was either her betrothed Prince Cowan or he was not. He was either deceiving or telling the truth. He was either real or a liar.

Everything in her knew he was telling the truth.

She closed her eyes, bringing his intangible image to mind. He was about four inches taller than her. A lean, lanky body that moved with a scattered kind of grace, constantly redirecting his steps as he considered thought after restless thought. His black trousers and tunic had been ripped, not to indecent levels, but sufficient to reveal that an Abstephian's entire skin changed colors with their emotions.

He had been ... unexpected, and she couldn't stop looking at him or remembering him.

That is his face. His form. He is real.

He was dying somewhere in this land. Before Usilea could learn the outrageous plan Petar had imagined, he had disappeared while in terrible pain.

How could I have thought he wasn't real? She sat up in the bed, tucking the cushions beneath her. In truth, he hadn't spoken of himself much over the years. As she recalled, there had been complaints of chores he needed to do, musings over difficult lessons, a mention of a guardian or two who watched over him. Stories of adventures in a dangerous wood. Mostly, he had listened to her and spoken about topics of interest or study they both enjoyed. He hadn't wanted to dwell on his life.

And I needed someone to speak to concerning mine. After listening to many others talk, it had been so refreshing to have someone focused on her. Listening to her. Cheering her up, and respectful of when she needed time alone.

Her heart ached. He had been there for her. She had let him, had clung to him as a lifeline. Now he was in trouble and assumed she wouldn't care, that she wouldn't even try. She had seen the hurt in his eyes over the word "imaginary." All of those times he had insisted he was his own person, all of those times she had dismissed him easily. Teasingly.

Petar! I know you are real, and you are there. Please, return to me. I want to help you.

"… don't … cry."

Usilea gasped. His mental voice was weary, each word coming as though from a long distance. But he was there, speaking to her in her mind.

Or was it in her room? Her head snapped around, trying to discern his location in the dimness. She always slept with a few dimly lit torches. A security precaution as well as a method for keeping away the nightmares from what she had seen her parents do to Menders.

No pale figure broke the darkness.

A dry chuckle sounded in her mind.

"No, goldenbird. I am … not there. It has taken … all my strength to … to be here with you as we always have." She could sense the sly turn of his thoughts. *"Besides, would it not … be scandalous … for the young, guileless, innocent queen to host … a man in her room at night?"*

She rolled her eyes despite her worry. *A scandal indeed. Although*

I have overthrown my family, so clearly nothing is beyond my grasp.

"Nevertheless, your reputation … remains intact." His words at last seemed to come more smoothly. "When I watch you—"

Can you not see me when you speak in my mind?

"Only the shadows and outline of you and the objects around you. Except when I manifested earlier … I saw you as clear as the morning sky after a rain."

A pleasant shiver wove up her spine at his words. Belatedly, Usilea remembered how he had stared at her during the funeral as though he could not look away. As though she were the only person in the entire world.

She inhaled. *Finish your sentence.*

"Beg pardon?"

When you watch me—how were you going to end that sentence?

Silence fell. For a moment, her heart sank.

Had he left once more?

"When I watch you worry in your bedchamber, it would only be as one who lays in bed next to you, assuring you that all will be well. Or else, distracting you from your fears." The pronouncement was a whisper, laced with desire and longing so tender it took her breath away. She knew Petar as her childhood confidante, growing into her dearest advisor. Never had she considered him as more.

No, that was a lie. She had longed for him as more, but it was a quiet, foolish yearning without hope. Now, as Usilea considered his words, her mind spun. He was her betrothed. He existed apart from her. He could someday be touched with her hand or even kissed— she swallowed, tracing her fingers over her lips.

"Yet, I speak out of place." His tone turned brusque. Was he embarrassed? Did he think she didn't share his feelings? Usilea searched for words to say, but he rushed ahead. "I am here, for I did not want *you to worry. I wander through mazes fierce, through forests strong, but ever I have returned to the side of the silver queen, the starlight queen herself."*

I'm glad. Very glad. Stones! Why couldn't she answer him so beautifully? If they were communicating through the written word, perhaps she could equal his lyricism after some time, but not with conversation.

There was something she could do. *I'm sorry, Petar. For believing you were imaginary. All of these years, you insisted you weren't, and I dismissed you countless times. It was hurtful and it denied your right to exist as yourself. It was rude and—*

"I forgive you."

I want you to know that I care about you, and I—you forgive me?

"What else would I do? The words were harsh, but you didn't know any better." His voice gentled again. *"You're my closest friend as well. What would I do without you capturing my wayward thoughts, giving value to my ideas, and somehow seeing me as ... more?"*

Her chest expanded at his words. Each one flowed deep within her like water, like air. With every word, she found her own soul more and more twisted in knots, her future shifting into new directions that she didn't know and had never anticipated. Everything was so sudden.

I will always see you. Usilea paused, chewing on her lip. If this was to be her new path, then so be it. There could be no other.

She turned in the bed and slid her legs over the side, her feet dangling just above the polished floor. *We should go to find you.*

"Now? It is late, goldenbird."

Astute as ever, clever boy. But it will be dawn soon, and there are preparations to make. How can I sleep any longer in this palace when I know you are out there suffering? Dying? She slipped the rest of the way off the bed, tied a robe over her nightdress, and padded over to the nearest lamp, turning up the wick brighter to illuminate the room. Then she walked over to one of her bags and withdrew a fresh sheet of paper and a new pen. *I'm a Mender who heals other Menders. Maybe that means I can help you as well.*

His aversion was clear through their bond. *"You aren't supposed to Mend."*

I'm not supposed to Mend much. A rule I made, so it is mine to break.

"A rule you made with your brother, sister-in-law, and the priest Ertax Valtor after much discussion about your unique gift. You are the queen. Putting yourself in a place where you Receive the harms of others leaves you vulnerable in a way you cannot be. You must lead your people." His correction was all the worse for how mild and matter-of-fact it was.

Could he not see that she—that he—could not—? Usilea pressed the nib of the pen into the paper with such force that it pierced a hole. She sighed a whisper of frustration and determination into the darkness of the room.

Those of us who have gifts must use them for the good of others. I will not dishonor mine by withholding it, least of all from you, my—

"Your what?"

My betrothed. The stirrings of her heart yearned for his soul, but to speak of it seemed as impossible as this entire situation. Moreover, if she spoke, if she admitted that she sought him for—no. Not yet. The words remained trapped deep within her. Waiting for what she did not know. *You are my betrothed, and we are to be married. Please, tell me everything you know about your physical location so that I can find you.*

"Are you truly—" He paused, as if working to keep up with her

words. *"I shall also do my part to be visible outside so that I can show you. Braierleve is a dangerous forest."*

I know, with many mazes and twists. Her lips quirked.

"And monsters beyond natural making, and thornflowers as tall as trees and as venomous as an assassin's poisoned arrow."

This is the place where you were raised? She remembered his stories, that were more than stories.

"Indeed it was. Although I believe it's more dangerous now than it was in my youth." Wariness edged his words. *"You do not have much experience with such travels."*

He was trying to be gracious. She had no experience with such travels. Jaric was the one who favored rugged terrain and isolated journeys to the middle of unspoiled forests. He had met his match in his wife Renna, who had been raised in the wilds of the north.

Usilea only squared her shoulders. *Then I am relieved that I will have an excellent guide.*

"Indeed. Can you trust any of your guards to allow you to leave?"

I am their queen.

"Exactly." His words were flat and direct and horribly practical. *"You are their queen. The queen. A queen does not simply dash off into the most deadly, ancient forest in Absteph after her imaginary friend."*

She glared into thin air. *You are* not *imaginary—*

"I'm well aware. If I were dead, it wouldn't hurt so much." A shadow filled her mind at the last words, but before she could ask after them, Petar continued. *"I have other ideas."*

Usilea sat back in the chair, her lips twitching with amusement and irritation. Both blessedly familiar and neither of which she ever wanted to be free of any more than she wanted to be free of him. *Go ahead.*

"Our new friend Larkin seems to want distraction. She also seems

sympathetic to our plight. Moreover, she is a Warper who can presumably transport you to various locations. You can remain here during the day, making your official visits of state with the Reign Lord"— he said the title with a sneer— *"which will allow us to detect any foul play among the populace. Then at night, once you retire to bed, Larkin can Warp herself within this chamber and transport you into Braierleve. There I can manifest and guide you as I am able for a handful of hours, and then she can return you to the palace."*

I am here for eight days. That doesn't give us much time.

"According to the Warper, I will die within five or fewer. Time is already short."

Her pulse jumped at his words. How could he be so callous about this? Although he had always taken that tone over the previous two years, as if something had happened to siphon his hope. When she had asked after it, Petar only said he couldn't remember the details, but he knew he was where he must be. She had accepted it at the time, believing her imaginary friend was starting to fade as she matured.

Perhaps now, if she traveled with him in this mysterious wood, she could awaken his memory. She could discover why he had become trapped. What had happened to his family.

"There is the matter of evading your guards, of course."

She frowned. *Indeed. Hmmm …*

"What is it?"

Silence, please. Usilea scribbled aimlessly on the parchment in front of her, trying to tease out the idea that seemed to fit so perfectly into their plan.

Ah yes. There it was. She smiled despite the dour situation.

I can merely say that we must consider appearances. What does it say to the people of Willowing Halls that the queen of Edrin doesn't trust their guards, so she must keep her own so close? They will be reassigned directly outside with my other two guards. Rilva and Pelreira would grumble, but they would obey their sovereign.

He gave a short, delighted chuckle. *"As always, your wisdom is beautiful. As is all of you."*

Words fled her. Petar had said such things before, but now that he had seen her, they seemed to take on fresh meaning. Having her imaginary friend believe her mind was beautiful was one matter—it had seemed narcissistic at times, which had always confused her.

To have her oldest friend believe her mind and form were lovely was another matter entirely. The declaration was rich with bold appreciation that nestled within her heart.

Thank you. That means everything coming from you.

"I only speak the truth."

A pause passed between them. No words uttered, no feelings other than a contentment mixed with a tingling sort of fearful anticipation. If they failed, Petar would be dead by all counts, not merely a cunning deception.

Usilea set her jaw.

It couldn't happen.

She would find him.

CHAPTER SIX

His people and his land were dying. Not as quickly as he was, but just as certainly. Ultimately, both would fall together.

Petar couldn't remember how he knew this so well, no more than he could remember his own location within Braierleve Forest. But the lack of memory did not make the knowledge less true. It only made it more difficult for him to share with Usilea. At this moment, she was otherwise occupied with her tour of Hicareth.

A visit that reminded him of how the Abstephians suffered. All were Makers of some kind, and all shared the gift, first among their families, then in their communities. Yes, there had always been some disturbances and unsavory characters, but the community allied with the guards to handle those matters. Everyone knew that their Making was tied to the land itself and the Eternal above. Petar recalled visits where every home featured verdant, well-tended gardens and sturdy homes. Some were nicer than others, some people had more abundance than others, but all had at least a solid dwelling and enough for each day.

Now, everywhere he turned were tall trees with decaying leaves, gardens with wilting plants, buildings with cracked mortar between the stones, and roads that were pockmarked with holes and unkempt edges. The faces of people were worn, their steps heavy, and their forms thin. Petar's lanky body had been unusual for his people, a challenge for his cooking guardian to feed. But now, everyone lacked substance on their large-boned frames. Their skin tones were bluish-brown and tainted with gray. Not the soft gray of rest, but the sickly gray of exhaustion.

"This is wrong. The royal family—my family—they would never have let this happen." His fingers ran over the crumbling thatch of a roof, not quite managing to feel it in his ghostly skin. "This should be treated with gelnas sap and formed carefully to dispel rain. I helped my house guardian do this in our cottage in the woods."

Usilea maintained her polite expression, even as her words filtered into his mind.

"*According to reports, Absteph has fallen prey to poor weather over the last year, which has affected the crops. Although there were rain showers this morning. Perhaps the soil is to blame? In any case, the royal family was unable to assist.*"

"But that is their role!" He glanced around, afraid someone might have heard. Of course, no one turned toward him. "They're the strongest, which means they must help others. It is in our laws."

"*Those were imposters, as you said yourself. Who knows how long the imposters sat on the thrones?*" They turned a corner to the Artisan Circle. As the area that held of some of the finest Makers, it should have been resplendent with expert craftsmanship and decorations. Instead, it bore the same decay as the general houses.

He swallowed hard. "And for a year, the country has had no true protectors from whatever taint this is that siphons away our vitrop."

"*Vitrop?*"

"The … life … no. The essence." Petar struggled for words. "It means we-and-land-and-sky-connection-share-alive-responsibility-heartness. That doesn't contain the full meaning."

Sadness coated her voice. "*I understand. Remember, my prince, since those who are dead were imposters, your family might still live somewhere. All is not lost.*"

"Now *you* comfort *me*." His lips twitched. "Forgive me, I distract you."

"*You do, but your home is in peril. I understand this. And I would rather speak with you than …*" For a brief moment, the faintest crinkles around her golden eyes revealed her annoyance. Then her features smoothed once more as the Reign Lord spoke.

"This, Your Majesty, is the Artisan Circle." Lord Aeson gestured toward a small collection of dwellings with a flourish of his fine black-and-silver robes. "All of our people have some measure of the gift of Making, but the artisans have far more than most—except for the royal family, Eternal watch over their souls."

Usilea's expression turned appropriately sympathetic, and indeed, the grief in her eyes was real. Within her quietude, she always had a heart for the struggles of others and a desire to see them made right with her power.

Each house displayed the skill of the family that inhabited it. The Makers gifted in stone had crafted intricate reliefs on their home, while the Makers gifted in cloth-work had draped their windows in dazzling fabrics with deep, rich colors. Yet, as they came out family by family and greeted Usilea, Petar noticed their sunken cheeks and brittle hair. They might be dressed in finer attire, and the Reign Lord insisted that all within the kingdom had ample food, but their movements were slow and wearied.

A woman wearing a golden-brown cotehardie stepped forward,

holding out two ends of frayed tapestry that had been ripped. She held them together and rubbed her bare fingers on the pattern, her eyes narrowing and her skin turning a deep orange-rose for a moment. The frayed edges wove themselves together under her fingers in brief starts and sputters until at last the piece was whole.

"Here you are, Your Majesty." The woman's shoulders slumped and her skin turned bluish-brown again with the effort. "A wall hanging for your house."

Usilea smiled and took the intricate fabric with great care. "It's beautiful. Thank you for your kindness."

"It should be so much quicker, so much easier for her to Make this fabric." Petar shook his head, his heart sinking.

The woman continued speaking for, of course, she couldn't hear him. No one could, save Usilea. "From our house to yours. As was …" Her voice faltered. "As was once to be."

"And, perhaps, will be again," Lord Aeson said, stepping forward and placing a hand on the woman's shoulder. "All is not lost."

At his words, something hot rose within Petar. "I'm not dead yet!"

His betrothed smiled faintly. *"No, you are not. You are mine."*

The soft surety in her words cooled the fire even as she spoke aloud. "Indeed, Reign Lord Aeson. Even if the marriage alliance is now out of reach, the country of Edrin is open to other types of alliances."

Aeson's skin took on a greenish-red tinge that quickly disappeared. The colors of anger and envy, a sharp answer to her sweet diplomacy. "We will have more conversations about this, I'm certain, Your Majesty."

"As you say."

At her words, Petar smirked. He had seen so many others underestimate Usilea over the years. They always rued the day they did so.

Another artisan beckoned them to view an ornate relief on the side of their house. Before the queen, the stoneworker used his bare fingers and his Making gift to turn a fragment of raw stone into a tiny basin with an elegant pattern. As with the fabric Maker, the stone Maker seemed exhausted by his small effort.

Furthermore, there was the matter of the relief work on the house. Petar could see how it was chipped and the paint was fading. What could have stopped the family from repairing such damage? They would have, out of pride as well as duty.

"I give everything I have, and still they languish." A pang of grief shot through him, as real as physical agony.

"What do you mean?"

He shook his head.

"I don't entirely know. Attend to your most devoted servant, the Reign Lord." Acidity touched his words despite himself. Admittedly, he didn't try to censor the strange, bitter feeling. "He is shrewd. A snake on equal with your parents."

Petar's jaw worked. An image surfaced. The Reign Lord, then only Lord Aeson, glaring at him. Daring him to take any action, even as the gold-green vines with needle-bared tips grew ever closer.

He acted. Oh yes, he acted, and the Reign Lord's howls of rage were music to his ears. Though it sacrificed that which he had always longed for, what he had so recently realized was his, he would do it again. They were worth every spark of life he had to give.

Sudden agony shot through him, this time from the tips of his fingers through his veins. Fire and lightning jolting through him, weakening him. Petar sucked in a breath, feeling his hold on the world around him fade.

"Petar!"

"I will see you tonight, goldenbird."

For unknowable time, all he felt was the pain arcing through his body, forcing him into shudders and spasms on some hard surface. Taking something precious from him, something that he fought to keep with every breath so he could pour it out to others.

At last he sagged back through the surface into it, below it to the ground or some other nebulous place. The torment was over, drifting away from him like a cloud. There was only the quiet. The dark sky above him through the rippling trees.

The familiar draw of her as a beacon in the night. No matter her feelings or whatever stood between them, he would be by her side as much as he was able. For there was no one else.

Petar stood in the layers of leaf litter, clad in the same ripped clothing as before when he manifested. Apparently, that was something he could not change. Attempting to do so would be as futile as trying to remember how he had withstood Lord Aeson or for what cause.

Mysteries lost to the abyss, into the hands of the Eternal. Whether or not he was always devout, he never doubted the presence of the deity. One didn't cast themselves into the depths, into the mystery of whatever he had done, without a deeper reason behind it. A deeper belief in someone greater.

A rippling sensation tugged at the moonlit shadows in front of him. The next moment, the air itself seemed to part and fold back like a blanket. Two individuals stepped through. One wore a yellow-flowered tunic that ended at her hips, brown trousers, a blue corset, and high black boots. He recognized the chin-length hair, glimmering gear ornaments, and mirkish smile of the Lady Larkin.

The other person had her black hair bound away into a knot atop her head, her shorter figure clad in black trousers and shirt with a corset overtop, along with a cloak and sturdy boots with thick soles. Golden eyes gleamed in the darkness. His—Usilea. She was here.

And judging from her expression, she was slightly annoyed at him and largely relieved.

He stepped forward. "Well met by moonlight, queen of the stars and sun. You look resplendent as usual."

Indeed, the more form-fitting garments were very compelling. He averted his gaze to her eyes as soon as he realized he was staring. Usilea had complained of men studying her like something they might devour. He had already been plain about caring for her. There was no need to jeopardize their friendship by revealing his full level of attraction.

"Well met, lord of nightmares." Her lips twitched into a small smile. *"I hope this forest does not disappoint. If I'm not alarmed within thirty minutes, I will be much dismayed."*

Petar grinned. Oh, he had missed her. "We will see. Sometimes the very thing you desire can be out of reach. Monsters dislike being ordered around."

"Then what good is it being a queen?"

"There must be some perks."

"I will let you know when I'm aware of them. Currently, it seems to involve entirely too much listening to men who are full of their own importance." Similar irritation to that of earlier filled her expression, making it clear she spoke of Lord Aeson.

Usilea turned to Larkin. "Thank you for bringing me here. Please come get me in five hours."

"No, three hours," Petar countered.

"That isn't enough time."

"We have other days. If you fall asleep in front of the Reign

Lord, he will be suspicious."

Usilea turned a pleading expression on him. *"Each day brings us closer to your ... "* She swallowed, fear overtaking her mild face for a moment. "Four hours."

"For tonight, at least."

"We will see."

Larkin nodded. "I'll show up after four hours, then."

"Will you be able to locate us?" Usilea asked.

"Not a problem. Your friend's ripples are getting stronger, especially in this area. I'll be shinning around in the meantime. Goodbye!"

Larkin seemed to fold the blankets of the world around her again and then vanished, leaving the two of them alone in the night.

"Well, goldenbird. Shall we be about it?"

She nodded. "Lead the way, lord of nightmares. I wonder, how have you earned that name? Through inflicting them on others or enduring them yourself?"

"Perhaps I will tell you on our search." Petar gave her a thin smile. "There might be some who consider me a nightmare."

"Not me." Her hand reached for his arm, barely sinking through the wisps of his manifested skin, as though her presence somehow pulled him back together. It evoked a curious, pleasant shudder through his form. "Never me, Petar. You are the light in the darkness, as you always have been. I will not let the shadows swallow you up."

His chest tightened at her words. Not flippant words, nor the silly teasing that they enjoyed, but deeper and filled with an intense emotion that he could not name, only hope for.

"Likewise, my goldenbird." He raised his hand as if to stroke her face.

Something whipped out in the emptiness behind her.

Clawed and barbed on a flicking tail.
Aimed at her throat.

CHAPTER SEVEN

The air whipped around her.

"Get down!" Hands that were half-evanescent pushed her to the ground. Usilea rolled with the movement, crouching low.

She had enough experience with her guards to understand letting someone protect her rather than protesting. Petar knew these woods far better than her, and he didn't give commands unless he believed there was no other way.

Nevertheless, she reached for a dagger within her cloak.

In the shadows, Petar fought against a monster with far too many teeth in a gaping mouth and writhing, furry limbs. Her betrothed's jaw was set in a firm line, but his lips twitched and his mismatched eyes glinted with a strange satisfaction, as if here, at least, he knew his enemy.

A moment later, a shriek like a rusty gate and a screeching child ripped through the air. Some things that were hairy and barbed hit the ground around her.

"Guard your face," he ordered.

She ducked within the confines of her cloak. Something wet

and misty hit it. The scent of rotting meat and old undergarments filled the air for a moment, then quickly dissipated.

"Will it damage the garment?"

"No, it shouldn't. The venom sacs quickly lose their stench when exposed to air." His voice gentled. "The area is clear now, but we must move on. Others will come to eat the corpse."

Usilea swallowed down bile and rose to her feet, spreading out her cloak. "Well, um, we will not disturb them, then."

By some grace, her voice was mostly level. She had seen horrific things before due to her parents' vile practices with the bodies of Menders, but that was a cold comfort.

"Come. I'll show you how to navigate safely." Petar reached out for her hand, clasping it with his own. Even though it wasn't firm, she still found it wonderfully present and necessary. At the same time, she felt lightheaded, as though she were taking on a measure of his insubstantial existence. As if she were Mending him.

If that were the case, Usilea would keep the knowledge to herself. In this small way, she could help him, and her body would heal from the Mending swiftly enough. In addition, it helped her continue to see Petar fully.

She nodded. "Thank you for saving my life."

"Thank you for listening promptly. Others have hesitated and died in Braierleve."

"I trust you." The words came out simply, for they were true. She knew he considered her needs above his own. It was a reason Usilea had believed him to be imaginary.

"Good." His lips parted, then his mouth closed. Then opened again. "After all, I can't let anything happen to the miraculous silver queen of Edrin. What sort of friend would I be?"

"What sort of friend indeed." Did her words catch on that pivotal word? Perhaps a little. Hopefully he wouldn't notice.

She wanted him by her side forever. They were betrothed. He had made it clear he wanted to honor that commitment, but he did not urge her further. A part of her wished he would, yet she was grateful he did not. There were other, more important matters to consider, such as freeing him and learning the truth of the imposter royalty.

"Mind your step."

"What? Oh." Quick steps caused her to miss a patch of oddly glowing blue-green toadstools and small twinkling purple flowers. "Are they deadly too?"

He shook his head. "No, but they are pretty, and I prefer not to injure them if I can help it. That is the larate pairing, made of teala fungi and turqa flower. They're symbiotic and only grow in close proximity to each other. In our beliefs, seeing them is considered a sign that your love is true. They tend to emerge quickly when a royal betrothed couple is near, spurred by their connection to the vitrop."

"Have these done so?"

He knelt and studied the plants for a moment. "No, they have not. Although neither of us are connected with the vitrop."

She repressed a pang of disappointment. Why should she care if the land approved of her? Though it was Petar's land.

"I see. And that hideous creature?"

"A mumphlay. Night hunters who find their prey by scent. Usually they aren't bold enough to attack groups of two or more." He frowned, then released her hand. "You can walk more easily. Please, stay close."

"Always."

They continued onward. Petar deftly guided her around rocklike formations that unexpectedly snarled and bit. He warned of hanging vines that swayed with musical chimes before trying to wrap around someone and consume their flesh with toxic acid. Amidst all the savagery, there were a few more pairs of the teala fungi and turqa flowers. There were curious, sleekly furred creatures creeping among the tree boughs above them, bright-eyed, sweet-smelling, and, as her friend assured her, entirely harmless.

Her friend. Her betrothed. Save for his quick, direct explanations, he had been quiet throughout their journey. His mismatched eyes were ever watchful in the night as he glided deftly among the trunks, as though a ghostly pale spirit of the woods himself.

"How long did you live here? *Have* you lived here?"

"All my life, until the day my guardians told me of my true role and destiny. That was ... two years ago?" He frowned, seemingly confused. Then a darkly whimsical expression overtook his face. "Never to go, never to stray, forever the woods to make your stay."

His voice spoke with the customary mocking fluidity, drenched in sorrow. Usilea winced in empathy.

"Another riddle, clever boy?"

"Or a curse. Maybe a curse."

"How is this forest so verdant when the rest of Absteph struggles?"

Petar paused, considering the question. "I think ... it is due to me."

"How?"

"I am—" He sucked in a breath and glanced around. At what? The air seemed to merely shimmer. "Goldenbird, do you carry your short sword?"

"Yes." Her pulse hitched, and her hand reached for the pommel.

"Draw it. Now."

She unsheathed the weapon with silent ease, just as her brother Jaric had taught her. The sharp blade glinted in the moonlight, reflecting off the faint shimmering and revealing the shimmers as fine, tiny threads, crisscrossing over each other in a thousand tiny patterns. Lacy. Elegant.

"Nal spiders. They're deadly." Petar's voice was a whisper. "Catch too many on your skin, and you will be forever ensnared until ..."

His words stopped short. Usilea focused on taking the slowest measured breaths.

"Until what?"

"Until they gild fresh webs *with* your skin." He gave the tiniest of shrugs. "I'm not quite here enough to tempt them."

"What is the plan?" Usilea pushed away the horror of his words. She had enough terrors to haunt her sleep already.

"Slice through as many webs as you can. I will deal with the nal spiders."

"Very well."

Hefting her sword, she swung it at the shimmering lines of webbing. Her weapon flowed with the familiar patterns that she had practiced so many times in secret moments when her parents weren't aware. They preferred to think of her as their defenseless pawn. As the edge of her sword hit them, a faint sound pierced the air, a fierce sibilance of a thousand tiny shrieks that crawled up and down her spine.

"You are magnificent. Continue, my—continue."

Then the shimmering lines flickered. Usilea paused, her muscles tense, blinking against the sight.

"Does the webbing affect the eyes?"

Petar's face was grim. "No. Those are the spiders."

She tilted her head. "Are they so small, then? Why should they be feared?"

"... perhaps this is not the best time to say."

"Tell me."

He spoke quickly. "Let them too close and they will find their way into the tiniest orifices of your body. They must burrow beneath to remove the skin."

She swallowed, gritting her teeth against the trembles that threatened her skin. "Wondrous. Thank you."

Usilea swung her blade with fresh strength, every part of her intent on obliterating the shimmering threads. Faster and faster she moved, whipping the sword around. Their lives depended on it. Petar might be too incorporeal to be affected, but she would be. If she died, he would too. No one else sought him out. Only her.

I will not abandon him.

He was hers.

Even as her arms began to ache, the threads disappeared—only to be replaced with new threads. They flickered so much that she could barely see them. How were more spiders coming out?

"Petar, I don't think this is working."

His gaze never wavered, his eyes distant. "It goes exactly according to plan. Keep swinging."

"More are coming!"

"More will, as they must."

"As they must? What are you thinking?"

"Of too much." He raised his hands, his fingers tracing through the air in small, careful arcs. She hadn't seen the Makers do that earlier, but Petar had said they were greatly weakened and fatigued. He was a prince of the royal line. Was this one of their particular talents?

More threads shimmered around them, closing in. Almost touching her flesh.

Her heart sank.

"Petar!"

He gave a wordless shout, the arcing motions growing wilder. Shimmering web danced around his fingers. He stepped forward, pushing into it, his ruby quartz and sapphire eyes flashing between darkness and light, black and white, over and over.

The shimmers fell to the ground as suddenly as though they had all been cut at once. The flickers died with them. Usilea's chest heaved, sweat beading her forehead and down her back. Her fingers tight and painful as they gripped her sword.

"It is done." Petar's shoulders slumped, his face pasty. "I'm sorry."

"Why? The nal spiders are gone, aren't they?"

He gave a sardonic smile. "They are. Every last one is dust. This nest is no more. So it goes."

"So what goes?"

"My destruction." He pursed his lips. "We should continue on. There is only an hour left."

"Two hours." The retort came out wearily from Usilea. The look in his eyes suggested he saw her fatigue.

"We shall see, goldenbird."

They walked on. Her legs throbbed with every movement. Usilea gritted her teeth against the pain. When she lurched away to avoid one of the snapping rocks, she stumbled back, knocking against another tree. Pain coursed down her shoulder, and she hissed.

"Usilea—"

"Don't say it." She glared at him.

He rolled his eyes, then gave her a winsome smile. "Well then, shall we talk about our mysterious bond? For I know that Menders meet their fated person in their dreams, but it is not so with Makers."

"I am a Mender, though. A unique one with unique power." The tension in her face eased as he slowed his pace. She didn't want to leave his side. Not when the morning held more of Lord Aeson. "What of Makers?"

"We meet our true other half when we are children. We know them at first sight."

"Children? Is it … odd?"

He laughed. "At that young age, the pair are merely devoted friends, or sometimes enemies at first. The connection is as essential to us as the vitrop, but thankfully we are given many years to grow together. The families encourage this as well. There are very few instances of it failing."

"I see." Usilea frowned. "When did you see me? For at our betrothal—was that you?"

Petar's tone lowered as he cleared a path through clinging brush. The nearest leaves seemed to disintegrate at his touch. "No … my parents did not fully trust yours. We are a private people. They used a stand-in. Or so I was told at age sixteen, when they came to inform me that I was a prince of the royal family and not merely a keeper of the forest." His voice softened with warmth. "But I saw you from where I stood in the crowd. And I—"

"You what?"

"I knew you as soon as I saw you. Even though I didn't understand how or why, for no one told me I had met my betrothed. But I knew you, and very soon I loved you."

Time seemed frozen around her. Her mind ceaselessly spun through the words he had spoken. He loved her. He loved her.

He had always loved her.

"Goldenbird? Is something the matter?" Petar drew closer to her. "You stopped walking. You might not feel the same, but my words are true." Emotions flitted over his face, bluish violet in color. Anxiety. Devotion. Love. "Considering the current state of affairs with my possible, ah, untimely death, I wanted you to know that. Yes."

Was she breathing? She needed to breathe because then she could speak to him. Then she could tell him the words that lay tightly knotted within her.

"I—I also—"

Leaves crackled near her.

"So, are you ready to leave?" Larkin interjected.

Usilea jumped, falling awkwardly on her ankle. She shook the pain out of it.

"Are you all right?" Petar studied her with concern.

"I'm fine." Of all the times to turn into a knock-kneed pup!

"I didn't mean to startle you." The Warper stood near an open rip in the air, her hands on her hips. "I know you said four hours, but I've heard stories about this forest, so I figured it was a better idea to come sooner."

Usilea was not usually a violent woman, but at that moment she almost could have ... well, done something rather painful to Larkin that she would have regretted later. She inhaled, then exhaled slowly. Tears prickled at the corners of her eyes.

How could all of this be happening now?

It was too much, far too much to cope with. And stones! She was exhausted. Every muscle in her body seemed made of lead.

"Thank you, Larkin," she said finally. "Your words are wise." She turned to Petar, the knots in her stomach twisting ever tighter. Maybe if she was alone, but—she barely knew Larkin! "I ... um. I agree."

Larkin tilted her head. "To what?"

"We should go now." Before the storm within her exploded in a most unseemly manner that she was not ready for. Not ready for at all.

Her betrothed's eyes glinted. His aura beamed of humor and concern. Did he not understand her? How could he? She'd said a random assortment of words!

Before she could think on it any further, Larkin grabbed her arm and pulled her through the rip in the open air. A strange, bath-like warmth flowed over Usilea for a moment, like in their earlier journey. The next moment, she was in her bedroom at the Willowing Halls.

"Well, here we are." Larkin released her arm and brushed off her dress, then yawned. "I can stay up the same as the next person—sleeping's not easy for me, actually—but I think I could manage a nap."

Usilea nodded absently. "You may go."

"Same time tomorrow, then." The Warper eyed her curiously, rubbing at one of the gears at the corner of her eyebrows. "Why didn't you just kiss him?"

"What?" Her head snapped up. "What do you mean?"

Larkin shrugged, crossing her arms over her chest. "He's meant to be the long-lost youngest prince, isn't he? News travels among nobles. You were betrothed to him—are betrothed to him. He's dying. You keep staring at his Warp disturbance ripples like a lonely dove. Except you left him all stiff and awkward."

Of all the impertinence! The knots within her stomach exploded into fury. Usilea glared at her, keeping her voice deadly angry. "He said he loved me. I was about to speak, and then you interrupted me."

"Hold your words!" Larkin raised her hands, her fair skin flushing. "I was only showing up early to help. I thought you might be tired."

"Yes, but … ohhh." She groaned and grabbed a cushion off the bed, holding it tightly. "I've never spoken those words before, not in that way. I didn't know what to say." Usilea sighed, the movement deflating her anger. "I'm sorry. This is all quite new, and I don't even know you well, but … I don't have anyone else to talk to here. Even at home, I have so few."

Never trust anyone, Usilea. They are only waiting for the opportunity to strike. She pushed away the warning, spoken early and often by her parents.

She would be careful, but she had to trust, no matter the fear within her.

The Warper nodded, her face softening with sympathy. "I understand."

"You do?"

"I'm from Nyark, but my father is from Sukei. The House Kwen allied with the House Throgmorton in an arranged marriage. I get treated differently at home, as though I'm exotic. Especially right now, when there aren't any other Warpers my age who aren't native to Nyark. It's a bit of a problem, and it's why I don't speak 'like a noblewoman.'" Her aura turned as sour as her expression. "Since I'm already treated differently, I might as well speak differently. My father doesn't like it. He's always wanted me to fit in and be the ideal Nyarkian citizen to gain respect for our family and to honor my late mother." She stepped forward and kicked at the edge of the bedpost. "At least your betrothed adores you, unlike mine."

Usilea sniffled, swiping at a few errant tears. "You're betrothed? You don't have a destined spouse? Someone else with your gift?"

Larkin rubbed her chin. "One time, we did. At least, that's what the books say. But our Houses didn't like being constricted. Officially, they wanted to give Warpers free will to choose, but I think they just wanted the freedom to make their own deals. So no, none of that for at least three generations. Nothing switches on anymore—wherever it would switch." She tapped her head, then over her heart, and then threw up her hands.

"Oh. And your betrothed doesn't like you?"

"Well, I thought we were getting on famously. Lord Virgil Emherst, a grand nobleman. It's an honor for my house and for his." Larkin's face turned a bit dreamy. "He's handsome and a skilled dancer. He's also a new arrival to the houses of Warping. Virgil inherited from his cousin after growing up in obscurity, so others fawn over him while making trouble behind his back. We connected over being outsiders and creating mechanical things and well, I thought it was fine. But recently ..." She tapped at her leg. "He's been distant. Cold. He was always arrogant and harsh about the nobility, and I dislike them myself but ... he's kept himself from me for months and ignored every letter."

Her mournful tone evoked sympathy from Usilea despite herself. "I am sorry."

"Me too. I didn't know a single person could make you hurt so much." She swallowed, lines tightening around her mouth. "The arrangement is for the best. Maybe he's just having a difficult time of things. Or maybe this is his true nature but if so, I wouldn't be the first lady in a loveless marriage. So I travel more as well, doing some unofficial goods trading on the side."

"At least it is easy for you."

"Indeed. Very easy. The nobility here really do like their tea, and for all that they're standoffish, they don't have nearly the fussy customs of the houses of Warping." Larkin's eyes twinkled, then she began moving toward the door. "If there's nothing else—"

A sudden thought occurred to Usilea. "You're a Warper. You have a gift."

"That's right."

With Larkin, she could test her idea of healing other gifted individuals, not only Menders. If she dared ask. Usilea pressed her lips together. Petar's life was at stake. She had to try. "Can I try Mending you?"

"You can do that? I've heard Menders can't heal other Menders. I thought it extended to the rest of us too."

Usilea sighed. "My parents committed unseemly acts to extend their lifespans, which granted me a different sort of Mending. But I've never had the opportunity to try and Receive a wound or ailment from someone with a different gift. If I can heal you, maybe I can also heal Petar."

"Ah, I see where you're headed." The Warper shrugged. "Would a tiny cut work?"

"That would be perfect because I could heal from Receiving easily enough."

"Well and good." Larkin pulled out a tiny dagger and poked the sharp tip into her index finger. Then she held it out, a bright drop of blood gleaming underneath the dim torchlight.

That was fast. Then again, the woman from Nyark didn't seem the sort to hesitate. Usilea swallowed and reached for Larkin's hand.

"For this to be most effective, I need to look into your eyes."

Larkin nodded, staring down at her. "Do your best. I'd rather not have to find a wrapping for my finger."

"I'll endeavor to save you the trouble," Usilea said dryly.

One moment she was falling into Larkin's dark brown eyes, feeling the energy of her lifeblood and Receiving the harm into herself. The next, she was blinking and pulling away. Pain prickled her finger. She looked down to see a tiny wound on the soft, lighter brown pad. The small injury was already healing.

"Will you look at that." Larkin stared at her finger. "Incredible." She rubbed at the fully healed spot, then cleared her throat. "Well, I should leave you to rest, Your Majesty."

"Usilea."

"Hm?" The other woman paused.

She gave a small smile. "You can call me Usilea."

An answering smile stretched across her new friend's face. "I will. Goodnight."

When the door closed, Usilea stripped off the exploring clothes, cleansed herself at the wash basin, and crawled under the covers, savoring the comfort of her nightdress and the blankets.

Petar? Are you there?

No answer. She grimaced. He had been visible throughout their journey. Perhaps he was exhausted. Or enduring terrible agony.

Usilea set her jaw. Next time he arrived, she would tell him how she felt in no uncertain terms. Then she would set about Receiving his wounds and healing him.

She would save him. No matter what.

she stares into the silent shadows
waiting for his voice
longing for his presence

but there are only the shudders
of broken dreams
and shattered edges
of a soul
too long
expected
to carry the weight
of the world

CHAPTER EIGHT

Sunrise came. No comments from Petar in her mind, nor any sight of him as she ate breakfast at a long hall filled with tables. It was Abstephian tradition to share the first meal of the day communally. Nobility ate at polished wooden tables according to their families, and since there was no other rulers, Usilea sat alone at a round table at the end of the hall. From her studies, there was a custom of inviting others to dine, but she couldn't remember it. No one invited her either, but that was no matter. She wanted to eat alone.

Usilea barely managed half of her serving of bread pudding and seared, brined meat strips. She only ate that due to her exertion the night before. The winey-sweet charberry juice caught in her throat with every sip. She could barely swallow.

Where was he? Had Larkin been wrong? It was only the third day. They had two more.

Two more seemed far too short. He was suffering, dying. And she was apart from him, enduring the unwanted attentions of Lord Aeson.

Politics maintain the order of kingdoms. I have a responsibility to my people.

Usilea sighed, staring at the embroidered panels of heavy, quilted fabric draped over the stone walls.

What of my responsibility to my heart? Moreover, what of Petar's claim to be the true prince, his belief that his family might be alive? She had a duty to help him as well. Shouldn't that duty take precedence?

"Your Majesty, are you well?" Lord Aeson's voice broke through her thoughts. He stood over her table. Irritation filled her. His absence had been small boon of that morning. "I regret that I was unable to join you this morning. Heavy matters of state stole my attention from your side."

She managed a faint smile. "I assure you that I survived."

"Indeed." He sat next to her, leaning in too close for her liking. "I'm pleased to see that the nobles abided by my decree to leave you in peace, even in my absence."

"Your decree?"

"Yes. Otherwise they would have been obliged to invite you to their table."

A stone settled in her stomach. "Reign Lord, is this the reason that no one has invited me or you to their tables previously?"

"Yes. I wanted nothing to interrupt our time together. I must confess, I delight in your company without intrusion." He gave her a long once-over.

She pressed her lips together, letting her anger flicker into her tone. "I came here specifically to share condolences with you and your *people.*"

Not that Usilea had been of any mind to do so that morning, but the fact that he forced others away was odious.

"Your kind heart is welcome and delightful, but I assure you, this is a better way. The custom of invitation is most unnecessary. Unlike the previous rulers, I do believe everyone should stay in their rightful places." Lord Aeson's aura radiated benevolent condescension. "You will indeed meet more of the populace. You will learn of their terrible plight with the drought."

"Good. I am ready." The words issued from her mouth with practiced ease, and she rose gracefully. Clenching her fist, then releasing it. For one day more, she could fill her role.

Eternal, watch over Petar.

The event for the day was a horseback ride over the plains to the east of the city where farmers tilled the ground. Naturally, the Reign Lord rode at her side, taking every opportunity to lean closer and tell her of the types of struggling crops and the history of the land. At least avoiding his flirtatious attempt to brush her hair out of her eyes kept her mind distracted from worrying over Petar.

For Petar was hers, even as she was his. Usilea frowned. She had made no offering of herself, other than her offer to heal him. Stones, she did so poorly at this game!

"Your Majesty, what do you look at with such disfavor?" He turned to her as their horses maintained an easy walk between two fields, their guards traveling at a deferential pace on their own mounts.

Usilea pressed her lips together, then curved them into a faint smile. Perhaps she could gain information another way. "I am only dismayed, Lord Aeson, that your people are frail, and your crops are still poor. Is there anything my people can do besides our shipments of relief food?"

He pulled away, his skin tinging faintly greenish-brown. With displeasure? It aligned with his aura, though his pleasant expression never wavered. "As I have said earlier, Your Majesty, the people are grieving."

"What of this … oh, what is that word?" She tilted her head in a winsome manner, then continued. "The virtruse? Oh, no … viretip? I remember learning it from somewhere …"

"The vitrop." The Reign Lord blinked once, then nodded. "You might be thinking of the phrase 'As it is with the land, so it is with the kindred.' A wonderful adage. A statement of folklore. Not truth."

A lie. Usilea knew that without requiring Petar's voice at her ear. Although she would have given everything within her to have him there, to feel him close as he whispered to her. She pushed the thought aside. It could have no place in this present conversation.

"How interesting," she replied. "I hope your land begins to thrive after the years of small yields and difficult times."

"Your empathy is most generous." His face melted into a soft, yearning look, though his eyes remained calculating. "I can only hope that with your arrival, the hearts of my people will lift as well. The old family has passed on, Eternal's light shine upon them. It is time for a new family to dawn."

Her cheeks heated. "Absteph mourns their former rulers. According to your traditions, they will do so for some time."

"As they must. But it is the responsibility of myself, as their new leader, to look out for their future beyond the mourning." Lord Aeson's tone lowered as he leaned near her once more, halting his steed. "There is no one superior to you, my queen."

Her fingers gripped the reins. How could he be so bold? His attentions were plain, but to suggest she abandon her people?"

"Reign Lord, I have my own country to oversee. A country that I love."

"As you should." He paused, adjusting his black and silver tabard.

"You have not been crowned yet. You also have an elder brother who has produced two heirs and who is a hero of many battles. In my own humble opinion, you could do well to expand your kingdom's horizons at my side."

"Do you mean together?" It took everything within her to quell the roiling in her stomach.

"Naturally. You overthrew your parents, an admirable achievement itself. You also have much to learn about life, and"—he gave a sly wink—"I have much to teach."

Usilea's back stiffened and she set her teeth. How had he managed to suggest she was unfit, attempt to appeal to her supposed ambition, and make a crude insinuation, all at once? "You are clever with words, Lord Aeson."

"Thank you, my queen."

"We have a phrase in Edrin. 'Fine futures lead to fiery ends.'" She clicked her tongue at her horse to move it away from his.

His eyes narrowed. "A curious phrase. What does it mean?"

"You are the one who claims ancient wisdom. You can explain it to me." She smiled sweetly, nudging her mount into a trot, then a smooth canter, allowing the cold breeze to carry away the fury within her and the sound of any further words from the Reign Lord. At least she had managed not to spit in his face. Jaric would be so disappointed at her restraint.

She needed Lord Aeson to think he had a chance of winning her hand, at least for a few more days.

Until she could find Petar and discover the truth.

The remainder of the day passed with milder, less frequent conversations. Lord Aeson seemed to understand that he had overstepped and kept a respectful distance. However, after they returned to the Willowing Halls, he again tried to take her hands in the intimate leave-taking. She deftly avoided his grasp and resisted the urge to wipe her palms on her riding clothes until after they had parted ways.

Alone in her room, Usilea's shoulders slumped as though burdened by the weight of mountains. She was grateful for the Abstephian tradition of keeping the evening meal a simple affair, taken alone or with immediate family. This custom she could embrace.

Then she inhaled the scent of fragrant steam. Her gaze immediately fixed on a bronze tub of hot water. Her heart rose at the sight.

"Rilva? Did you call for a bath?"

"I thought it prudent, considering the length of the excursion." Her guard and servant moved into Usilea's field of vision. Rilva's face, grayish-brown shale with a tint of ruby-rust, creased into a grimace. "We all thought you could use some additional rest, Your Grace. Fending off the advances of that king is no mean feat."

Usilea winced. "You noticed that, did you?"

She unpinned her cloak and let it fall to the floor. Her garments quickly followed, as her other guards had remained outside for her privacy.

"His manner was not difficult to read." Rilva deftly tied Usilea's hair away from her face and wrapped it in a silk cloth. "He's different than the others here. The guards of this hall will hardly give one a look, never mind speaking. The famed Abstephian reserve you hear about."

She nodded, easing one foot, then the other, into the tub. "When I endeavored to engage the meal servants in conversation, it took several tries. Then they did speak and seemed friendly."

"Yes, they don't seem to mean anything by it. But that Reign Lord … I don't know. Watch out for him, Your Grace. A few of us had our hands drifting toward our crossbows near the end."

"It would be a political disaster to kill the future monarch of an allied country on a visit of state." Usilea settled back against the edge of the tub, exhaling. Her shoulders relaxed in the warmth. "And it would be cruel. Lord Aeson is rude and forward, but those aren't reasons to end his existence. Life is precious."

Rilva set a thick drying cloth on the floor next to the tub, then placed another cloth on a nearby chair. "My apologies, Your Grace. But mark my words, that man is trouble. He has no place trying to pursue our queen. You're worth far more than the likes of him."

"Thank you, Rilva." As comfortable as Usilea felt with her servant, agreeing to violent actions was never a good habit. There were many conversations that could only take place within the confines of her mind. A place where only one other could sometimes hear her words, and Petar would always reply with his own thoughts and feedback. She could trust him to offer wise counsel.

"I'll bring in a tray of food for your evening meal, Your Grace, and then be out of your way. A rest will suit me as well." Rilva's words signaled she would be off duty tonight. She certainly deserved to rest.

As the door shut behind her, Usilea let her mind drift into aimless thoughts, calming words from the texts of the Eternal, and then back toward her meeting with Petar in the woods that night. If it would even occur, since he had been absent for the entire day.

The reminder chilled her despite the warm water. Abruptly, she sat up and set her jaw. She needed to eat and prepare. After washing her hair and combing through it with jular oil, she wrapped it up and got out of the tub. Then she dried herself, used more of the oil on her skin, and dressed herself in underclothing and a robe. Rilva or another one of her female guards could have assisted her, but after the long day of attention, Usilea preferred to be on her own.

At last, she sat down at her desk with the tray of food, which consisted of slices of dark brown bread, a variety of pickled vegetables, a few small, smoked fish, a few slices of raw fish, and some kind of fruit jam. Usilea had found some of the Abstephian cuisine appealing, especially the cured foods. Still, a part of her longed for the fresh fruit and light buns of Edrin. And she steered clear of the brined hela root. It smelled like garbage.

At our wedding feast, I might request that be left off the menu. Her lips curved at the thought. Scarcely had she dared to think of their wedding ceremony or of what lay beyond. As queen, she would be expected to produce at least one heir. Would their child's skin glimmer with minerals like those of Edrin, or would it shift to different colors like someone of Absteph? The hair might be lighter brown, at least.

Or perhaps it would be entirely white-blond, like Petar's. Currently, his hair was a mess. Perhaps once she found him—for she would find him—she would help him clean it. *What do Abstephians use for their hair?*

"A rinse of herb water." His words were soft in her mind, as if touched with exhaustion.

Usilea startled. Her utensil fell from her fingers. *You are here.*

"Yes, I am. At last."

She turned to see Petar standing there, his face coated with a sheen of sweat and his clothing further ripped. Including his shirt, the front of which was in tatters, open enough to see that his chest was not injured, though the muscles were also coated in sweat.

Heat rippled through her. She bit her lip and focused on his expression once more. That angular handsome visage that belonged to a very real person. Her betrothed. Hers.

His lips quirked. "You are quiet. Did I interrupt your evening repast?"

"Oh! Oh, I mean, yes. You did, but I don't mind at all." Usilea's hands fluttered to her hair, which she had absently freed from the wrap while thinking. The strands were in complete disarray. "I am merely—food, that is. I am eating food."

"Yes, you are." Petar winked at her, then took a step back. "But you are in a dressing robe. I should leave—"

"No." She stood. "There is a screen I can use and … and you're alive. I was worried. You haven't been around, haven't spoken to me all day."

He frowned. "Have I not? Time moves so oddly when you aren't truly united with yourself." His right hand rose to his chest and he began pacing. "Some kind of animal tried to attack me. I don't remember which one, but …" He suddenly grinned and paused. "I think I remember where I was! I think … we could find me there. How has this never been possible before?"

Usilea swallowed and stepped closer to him. "I know why."

"You do, goldenbird? How?"

"It was me." She took another step toward him. Only the space of a person between them now. "I discovered last night that I can heal others with gifts, not only Menders. I was able to Receive an injury from Larkin. Which meant that earlier that night, when I held your hand, I was starting to Mend you."

His eyebrows rose. "You can? Clever of you." Then his gaze darkened. "You shouldn't have though. Queen of starlight, your life is too valuable—"

"My life is mine to give as I choose." Another step. Close enough that she had to stare up into his eyes, though only slightly, for he was only a few inches taller than her. Tall enough. Her breathing shallowed. All of her being, her hopes and fears and all else, rested on this single moment. "And I choose to give it to the one I love."

She reached out and rested her hand above his heart, almost feeling it through the evanescent contact. "I love you, Petar. I never want to be parted from you again."

His mismatched eyes, rose quartz and sapphire, stared down at her in wonder as his fingertips traced a faintly tangible trail over her cheek and down the line of her jaw. "My queen, my Usilea," speaking her name like music, "I would be with no one else for the rest of my life. However long I might have."

"I will make sure you have as many days as the Eternal wills." Stones, how she wanted to kiss him right now. "And that not one of them is stolen by—"

"He knows!" Larkin's sharp, clipped cadence broke through from where she must have Warped inside the room. "We have to go."

Usilea turned to her, irritation filling her. "Who knows?"

"Lord Aeson. I was just in his study—"

"Why were you in his study?" Petar's voice echoed above Usilea.

Larkin plowed on, unable to hear him. "—and he had a lot of books on the theory of gifts, and even how someone can take someone else's gift, which is odd, but then he came in with someone, so I hid in a closet to hear what he was saying. He talks to himself, which isn't evil in itself, but his words were." She sucked in a breath and exhaled it as a gust. "He did it to your betrothed, *he's doing it* to your betrothed, and Usilea, you need to get dressed because he's figured out that you might be healing the prince."

"Frostmelt," Petar exclaimed. "I knew he was treacherous."

Ice ran down her spine. Usilea immediately grabbed up clothes and ran behind the screen. She threw on the garments, hurriedly tying back her hair away from her face. There was no time for braiding or other treatments.

"Hurry!"

"I am."

Voices came from behind the door to her bedroom. Lord Aeson couldn't harm her, but he might raise enough of a diplomatic issue that she would have to sort it out. Then he would harm Petar.

Never. She emerged from behind the screen. Larkin's hand latched on to one wrist while her betrothed's ephemeral grip encircled the other.

They did this now.

Petar's nightmare ended tonight.

CHAPTER NINE

She loved him. Usilea loved him and wanted to be with him. When she had declared she would find him and always have him with her, she meant that she would honor their betrothal and they would be wed.

Because she loved him.

If I survive. He set his jaw. They would never be parted again. Petar had believed that giving up himself was all he could do to save his family, but if she wanted him, needed him, then being a king at her side would be his next calling.

Fingers snapped in front of him. His breath caught as he emerged from his reverie. Larkin stood before him, her eyes focused vaguely in his general direction and her expression peevish.

"Prince? I know you can hear me even though I can't hear you. We're in the forbidden forest of terrifying doom, and it's high time for you to direct us." She put her hands on her hips. "I don't know what tricks your uncle has in store for us, but as I said, he had some scary books in his study."

A faint pressure and warmth in his hand confirmed that Usilea held it. He squeezed back, wishing she could feel him more. Another reason to hurry, and to be grateful that she was Mending him even now. Though she shouldn't have to.

She turned, her golden eyes staring up at him. "Petar, can you remember?"

He frowned. "I know that ... Lord Aeson betrayed my family." He released Usilea's hand and began walking slowly back and forth in the small clearing where they stood. It was free of most hazards, for it had been subject to a horrific fire and the scars burned the earth. Petar wasn't sure how he knew about the fire, only that he did. "I had to stand against him and ... he takes from me. Somehow."

Usilea repeated his words aloud for Larkin.

"He's taking your gift," Larkin said. He paused to study her as she continued. "He wants it for himself."

Petar resumed pacing, trying to search his mind for answers. "The idea is abhorrent. Each is given their due measure. Since all of Absteph shares in the vitrop, what harms one will harm the whole."

"Which might be why the land suffers," Usilea put in. "You're of the royal line, which means you would be bound to the land. Harming you would harm the land."

"Yet I am only one person. Unless ..." He stopped again. "My family. He's also harming my family. No, he cannot!" Petar sought for memories of them. For some reason, they came faster, perhaps due to Usilea's healing touch.

He recalled playing with his siblings as a child, assuming they were merely being kind to him, then simply choosing not to think about why they were friends. He remembered lessons in his Making gift in Braierleve, which had been wasting away from the presence of foul creatures and blight when he had arrived, so bad was it that it had formed a separate connection to the vitrop apart from the rest of the kingdom. Then being brought to the Willowing Halls at age sixteen and told that he was, in truth, the youngest prince of the royal family, kept in hiding due to his extraordinary power, and was betrothed to Crown Princess Usilea of Edrin.

Remembered elation filled him. His closest friend could be his, and he could be hers. He would have to surrender his own country, but he would gain so much more.

Anger had joined the elation. His family had lied to him and sent him away. Though they believed it to be necessary, he had grown up as an orphan. How could he now be a prince?

"I ran from them. I wanted to spend time with my guardians and visit my home one last time," he muttered, running a hand through his tangled hair. "So much had changed, I just … why can't I remember?" A yell escaped him, echoing into the night.

"Very subtle, prince," Larkin retorted.

Usilea glanced at her. "You could hear that?"

"No, but the ripples around him grew stronger. Why don't you simply heal him more intensely?"

"I could," she replied, drawing out the last word thoughtfully.

"No," he said at the same time.

To incidentally relieve his ailments was one matter. But Usilea, taking the pain he bore on a daily basis? He opened his mouth to protest, but she pressed her hand over his lips. "No. It is as I said earlier. Even as I will be your queen, you will be my king. I will use everything in my power to help you. Those are my only conditions for our marriage beyond what is stated in vows."

She pulled her hand away, the exquisite garnet intensifying in her deep brown cheeks. She was in earnest—and irresistible. He sighed. "Very well."

Her lips curved briefly, then flattened with concentration. "In ordinary circumstances, I would simply take your hands and look into your eyes. I'm not certain if that will be sufficient since you aren't fully here at all."

"Nor do you know what will come of this action."

"Yes, but it is all we have." Usilea reached up once more, placing her palms on either side of his face. He felt light contact. Was it stronger than before? "I need you to reach out to me in turn, Petar. However that occurs for you, your soul must seek out mine as never before."

"I appeared in your mind and dreams across miles." He gave a crooked smile. "The queen of sun and stars asks for the entire world."

"I know." Her quiet sincerity leached away the remains of his humor. She breathed in deeply, then exhaled. "There isn't much time. Let us begin. Tell me when you start to feel or remember anything more."

Her palms seemed to warm on his skin, as though she were the sun melting snow from a long winter. Petar fell into the depths of her star, finding himself in the most slender, delicate ribbons of light. The smallest drops of heat in the cold of night.

He closed his eyes, following the drops of light to the shadows they slowly eroded, pinprick by pinprick. "I remember ... thorn-flowers."

"What of them?"

"They surrounded my home in Braierleve, planted as a protective barrier, for they carried a drop of my blood in their roots." Pain shot through his temples, then quickly vanished as it was Received by Usilea. He couldn't linger here. "Silver-white and silver-gold thornflowers rising up as I walked to the door."

"Who is there?"

He tilted his head, trying to focus on the image and not on his fears about what Usilea might be enduring. "Lord Aeson. He introduced himself as my uncle. He … he claimed to welcome me to the family, but the flowers rose higher in response and their thorns grew longer."

She gave a strained, distant breath. "And what happened next?"

"I met him with skepticism … then he … did something to me. The thornflowers turned on me." Agony stabbed through him. "I had no choice … ran to the torch within and …" Petar's eyes slid open. "I burned them. I burned everything to the ground."

Usilea drew her hands back from his face. Her skin held an ashen cast, and her shoulders were slumped with weariness. "What of your guardians?"

"I never knew. They were not present at the cabin." He shuddered. "I know—I know where I am."

An invisible rope tethered him to his physical form now, as tangible to his mind as anything in the forest around him.

Larkin looked up from where she was leaning against the husk of a fivit tree. She brushed at her red tunic and black pants and corset. "Oh, good! Take us there."

"You can hear me?"

"Looks like it."

"Yes, we must go." Usilea straightened, then teetered sideways. She swallowed hard. "After I regain my footing."

"Allow me, my queen." He bent down and lifted her up, one arm beneath her knees and the other supporting her back. Her weight was comforting and real.

She sighed, encircling her arms around his neck. "Thank you."

"Sprockets! I can see you." Larkin rubbed at her eyes, then surveyed him again. "I know why she favors you now. A little unkempt for my taste, but a sight to behold anyway."

Petar focused on Usilea. "How do you feel?"

"As though I've been struck by some kind of lightning. But it will pass. I will heal. And you are whole enough to carry me." She gave a small smile.

"I must thank you as well." He pressed a kiss to her forehead, which was clammy but firmer than it had been, and wonderfully alive.

"Come on, love-birds!" Larkin was now a few steps ahead of him, her sturdy boots crunching on the blackened soil. Then she doubled back to keep pace at his shoulder.

"As you say." He squared his shoulders and stepped into the depths of the forest, taking care to usher the Nyarkian around the fang-stones that bit and the tanglemoss that clung to skin and caused it to glow in the darkness. Useful at some times, but not when they were trying to move stealthily. "It isn't far from here."

Usilea had closed her eyes, and her lips trembled. The cost of rapid healing from Receiving another's wounds. He would have spared her that pain. Still, he could guard her from the forest.

"Consider this, Your Highness. If it isn't far for us, then it isn't far for your uncle either. He must have some way of tracking you or he wouldn't have caught on to our scheme." Larkin squealed as a rock lunged for her foot, then stomped her chunky heel. "Try that again, pebble, and I *will* smite you."

Petar's lips twitched then tightened into a thin line. Larkin's words cut true. There was no time to waste.

The moon had risen higher in the sky by the time they stopped. Usilea once more strode beside him at her insistence that she was much improved. He noticed the hollow circles that remained beneath her eyes but had no choice but to accept her words. The closer they moved to his physical form, the more the tether pulled at him, causing him to move faster as though urged by the very ground beneath his feet.

At last, he emerged in a small patch of cleared land surrounding a dense thicket of thornflowers. The plants grew twice as tall as him on thick stalks with many flowers in their drooping, dormant states. Likewise, the thorns were pressed smooth and flat against the stems.

"Where are we? Where is your body, prince?" Larkin studied the flowers. "Are those weeds going to bite us?"

"No. They emerge at dawn."

Usilea laughed shortly next to him. "Beware the thorns at sunrise."

"Indeed." He stepped toward the cluster of plants.

"I don't suppose anyone remembered to bring a sword? I only have this." A small dagger glinted in Larkin's hand.

Petar brushed away her gesture. "Sheathe that, Larkin." He saw Usilea reach for a long knife and shook his head at her. "They are no threat."

"How do you know?"

"My blood helps to feed them." He knelt, pressing his palm to the ground. "The vitrop binds them to me, especially in dormancy."

Move aside. A simple command. One he had learned as a young child.

The clusters of thornflowers bent aside, creating an archway of thick, heavy vines. Before him rose a pedestal four feet off the ground, an oval stone in the customary style of funeral rites. A prone figure lay across the top on his back, his black clothing ripped and matted, white-blond hair scattered around his face.

"Who is it?" Usilea whispered. He had not heard her move next to him.

"… me."

He took one step toward the pedestal. Then another.

"Petar, what are you doing?"

"What I must." There was no turning away. The tether was as sure and solid as steel, binding his heart and soul. No matter how he had tried to escape, to make a way out, it always found him.

Hands grabbed at his arms, tried to move him back.

It was too late. There could be no other path for him.

As soon as Petar stepped beneath the archway, the world vanished, replaced by his familiar friends of darkness and pain.

Within the confines of his form, he gave a silent, endless scream.

CHAPTER TEN

A strangled sound ripped from Usilea's throat.

He was gone. Vanished before her eyes. Within her heart there were only empty echoes where his soul had been.

"No." She glared at the archway before her. "*No.* You don't get to take him."

"Usilea—"

"No!"

She burst into a run straight into the archway, unconcerned about her fate except that she be rejoined with Petar.

As soon as her shoe reached the entrance, the bent-over thorn-flower stalks began snapping back into place. Petar's body was cloaked in murky, night-shadowed greens and grays.

"Wait, you can't just—"

Usilea ran faster, her heels digging into the ground. Her hand reached for her long knife, ready to take out any nefarious plant that stood in her way. She had cut down the tiny, deadly nal spiders earlier. She would stand against anything else in this forest that stood between her and her prince.

Halfway there now. Her breath came in rapid gasps. If she reached her love without air, at least she reached him.

Massive columns of stems loomed up in front of her. She gritted her teeth and skidded around them, only to crash into another thicket. Darkness descended from above. Even in their folded, dormant state, the massive blooms obscured the moonlight.

Usilea spun around, her heartbeat thudding in her ears and her hand gripping the handle of her knife. The plants were inches from her face, moving in closer and closer, hemming her in on all sides. The air grew thick and heavy. The thornflowers might not be a threat before sunrise, but their proximity seemed meant to suffocate her.

A handful of thoughts repeated in her mind.

Petar. Petar is out there. I must find him. We were so close!

Part of her knew she should inhale through her nose and calm her pulse. Assess the situation rationally and come to an intelligent solution, as her parents had taught her.

But somehow, the peace was gone. Missing, like the young man who held her fragile hopes within his blithe smile and scattered movements.

No matter how diplomatic she had been, how careful, it had all come to nothing.

For she was alone. Bereft of her family. Of even her imaginary friend.

The stems stood silent sentinel around her, imprisoning her love and stealing the breath from her lungs.

Was this the end?

"Augh!" She flung out her arm that gripped the knife. It sliced through the nearest stalk, drawing forth a spray of crystalline sap. The thornflower's small leaves fluttered in an unseen breeze. Usilea turned her face away from the spray. It could be as toxic as so many other things in this forest.

She slashed at another, and then a third.

More crystal-clear spray.

More leaf flutters.

But the stalks stood firm.

Her shoulders shook, and she swiped away the salty wet on her cheeks. What had Mother said?

Darling, tears are only in your favor if they can manipulate others. One of her many bits of wisdom, spoken in the kindest of tones.

Somehow, it never made them hurt any less.

More warm wetness clung to her fingers. Usilea glanced down, squinting in the darkness.

Blood smeared the underside of her hand. She must have accidentally hurt herself while flailing. She studied the smear absently. Numbly.

Blood. Petar had said something about blood. *They surrounded my home, planted as a protective barrier, for they carried a drop of my blood in their roots.*

Usilea stared around herself with fresh eyes. What else had he said?

My blood helps to feed them. A morbid idea, but one that could fit the Abstephian connection with the land. It seemed that thornflowers, above all else, protected royals when they were nourished by them. The foolish things were only doing as they were told. Moving according to their nature and purpose within the vitrop.

She was royal as well. From a different land, but also possessing a gift, one of Mending, of healing. Maybe of new growth as well?

Would the vitrop listen to her? It had acknowledged that she and Petar were fated by helping them meet across the distance. Destiny bonds were considered an ordinance from the Eternal himself.

If so, the vitrop answered to that same deity.

"There is one way to know."

Usilea knelt down, then eyed the blood on her hand. She clenched her hand and released it to bring out more blood.

"Please, let this work. *Please.* I don't have anything else."

She reached down and pressed her hand to the ground. A faint energy flowed up her arm. Almost … curious. Wondering about her.

I'm Usilea. Betrothed of Petar, of Prince Cowan. I am royal. I need to be where he is.

No answer. Only a vague sense of confusion. It reminded her of when her dog Opal received an unfamiliar command and tilted her head to the side. Attentive to her master but having no idea what to do.

Commands. Could it be that easy? She knew so little about the vitrop.

Usilea shrugged. It was worth trying.

Get me to him.

The only sounds were her own labored breaths.

One more time. She considered Opal. The labordrim responded best to very simple, specific words.

What did Usilea want the stems to do?

Move apart.

At once, she felt a shifting in the soil and looked up. The stalks were easing away and bending back, creating an archway similar to earlier. At the end was the oval platform with Petar resting on the top.

Usilea's mouth dropped open, and she rose slowly to her feet, hardly daring to exhale into the still air.

"Thank you."

No acknowledgement. If the stems, or the vitrop itself, were only of the intelligence of Opal, they wouldn't understand. Her hand had left the ground.

There was no time for further thought. She needed to save Petar.

Slowly she walked down the archway, giving quick, wary glances at the stalks above her. Then moving more quickly as she neared the platform until finally, she stood by his side once more.

He looked as he had in his ephemeral form, only his skin was bleaching white. He was close to death.

Long white-blond hair matted with dirt and dark red stains splayed around his face. Black pants and tunic ripped. Claw marks scarred his skin. She reached out hesitantly to trace one. How had someone gotten through the thornflowers?

Another royal. Lord Aeson was part of the royal family. Or perhaps he had inflicted these on Petar before his imprisonment.

Fury stoked embers within her. She pushed them away. The fury could come later, after she had Mended Petar.

Usilea leaned over him, resting her hands on either side of his face. Her fingers stretched out to uncover his eyes. Only blankness stared back at her. She focused on his sightless gaze more intently.

Nothing.

No soul to fall into, no depths to pierce with empathic knowing.

Her brow wrinkled. How was she to help him? What other form of connection? Stones, she knew so little about Mending!

Then her attention fell to his lips. Thin, sensuous. Eager to twitch into smiles or to move in conversation when he was awake.

It would be another point of contact. Another way to assure Petar that even while he lay trapped in nightmares, she was with him.

She would Receive his pain, for he was hers.

Before Usilea could think further, she tilted her head down and touched her mouth to his.

Gently. Softly.

Only seeking out the one that she loved to remind him that he was loved in return.

That he was not alone.

Can you see, oh queen of starlight?
What remains is all undone
Spinning around in endless ashes
A maze of mysteries unsung
A maze of agonies unspun—

No.

Lord of nightmares
Lord of rue
you are no lord fully
the phantoms lord over you
I can free you
if only
you trust my heart is true

oh my dearest lady
you know not what you speak
the terrors I have suffered
are never yours to take

you cannot prevent me
O lord of what you've lost
you must rise
and Make a world
where we can live
as one
rise, my lord

Rise!

CHAPTER ELEVEN

He woke to silence. To the face of the woman he loved, lined with sweat and tears and determination. Her hands cradled his face as she Received the painful tether that had kept him so long trapped—and then broke it apart.

"Usilea." His Usilea. He placed his hands over hers. "You are done here, goldenbird."

"I must ... I must heal ..."

Her shoulders slumped and her grip loosened. Petar gently eased her hands off his face and slowly rose to a seated position. She sat down next to him, her head sagging down against his shoulder, hair smelling of fragrant oil.

"You have, more than you realize." His voice sounded odd to his ears. Hoarse from lack of use, lower than before. How long had it been? Two years.

Two years of captivity, unable to even remember where he was or why he had been held captive.

Yet all he could think of was Usilea. His betrothed, who had come so far, who had never stopped fighting for him. Seeing him when no one else could.

"I love you," he whispered.

"And I love you."

Their hands found each other and locked tightly. Her deep brown skin against his gray-tinged flesh, as he was at rest. For once, truly at rest. Her gift of Mending hummed against him, but his own gift met it, keeping her from spending herself when it was not necessary. He was free, and the land welcomed him. Through the vitrop, it spoke to him without words, gave knowledge through quiet nudges.

His family lived. They too had been imprisoned in their own protective clusters of thornflowers. Lord Aeson's work, even as he had also masked their presence so none of their people could discover the truth.

Petar sighed. Could he ask Usilea for more when she had already given so much?

"What is it, clever boy?" She squeezed his hand. "Something troubles you."

"My family is also entrapped. I can sense them through the vitrop." He stood. "I must find them, but Lord Aeson hunts us, and you are fatigued …"

She likewise stood, her expression firm. "Then we will free them, together." He opened his mouth to protest, but she continued in her soft, steel tones. "They are my family too, through our upcoming marriage. Absteph is an ally of Edrin. It is my political responsibility to support the leadership when a usurper is attempting to take the throne."

"As you say." Warmth spread through him. There could be no arguing with her, nor would he want to. "Let us depart, my queen."

He waved his hand to make the archway widen and allow them

passage side by side. The stalks lagged as though they were still commanded by another. Dread knotted in his stomach, cutting through the pleasant haze of affection.

"Lord Aeson is near," he muttered. "We must hurry. As much as you are able, that is."

He gave her a concerned look. She only raised her chin.

"I am quite capable of healing swiftly, like any Mender."

Even so, they passed through the hall of thornflower stalks with brisk strides rather than the dead run that twitched at his limbs. After so long imprisoned, his voice might be out of sorts, but his body seemed ready to race up a mountain.

"It took you long enough." Larkin looked up at them from where she lay across the grass on a series of pillows, propped up on her elbows in front of a book.

Usilea huffed, her golden eyes glinting as they walked closer. "I see you made yourself comfortable."

She grinned. "Why not? I would have worried more, but there wasn't much I could do in any case. Warping can't breach that thicket. I tried." Larkin pointed to a small plate next to her. "Dried meat? Calla orbs? A candy, perhaps?"

"I will take all of those," his betrothed answered quickly. "As will Petar, I'm sure. He hasn't eaten in two years."

"She speaks the truth. Then we must depart. My uncle is near."

He accepted the fruit and other bits of food she offered, along with a flask of water. Items she didn't have to pack, for she could simply Warp to their location and take what she wished. A remarkably convenient gift.

"I know he's here. He's over that way some," Larkin said, scooping her book off the ground and tossing it casually into a bag. "You royals all seem to leave ripples in the space between realms when you use your gift. Even you, Usilea. Yours are very subtle. Lord Aeson isn't bothering to hide his ripples. Although I'm not sure why he didn't just try and attack you directly."

Usilea frowned. "Perhaps he fears us being together?"

"Likely." Petar began to walk around the empty plate as he thought. "We also might be farther away from him than I realized." He paused and looked at the sky. The moon was far higher. "Larkin, how long until sunrise?"

She looked at a timepiece strapped to her wrist. "An hour."

Frostmelt! "We don't have much time." He began to pace faster. "He preys on weakness. He wants power. He … he knows I'll return for my family."

Cold, certain anger filled him.

"Your family?" Larkin popped another piece of candy into her mouth. "Why them?"

Memories rushed into his mind. "They were the ones I was protecting. He wanted to siphon all of our magic, starting with me because I was so powerful." His heart sank. "My power was the reason my parents sent me away. I can access the vitrop more than any other Maker. Existing so close to the power of my family was harming the infrastructure of the kingdom and the stability of the ground beneath us, even causing the dormant fire mountains to smoke. A small child can't understand what to do with that level of power. Moreover, my family feared others would try to capture me." The words came out numbly now, as straightforward as he had heard them from the lips of his father, the king. "They sent me to Braierleve, a half-dead, diseased forest so infested it had been cut off from the rest of the vitrop. Even when I was young, I was able to create a small space for myself and my guardians to live safely."

Usilea's arm slipped around his waist. "Was that why you were betrothed to me?"

He nodded, caught up in the same hard emotions that had consumed him two years earlier. "They assumed I would never find my destined spouse because no one else could match my power. Moreover, they believed it was necessary for the safety of Absteph that I live away from it, and with my strong gift, they believed I would thrive in another land." He gave a rough exhale. "As soon as my uncle ambushed me, I felt weaker and was unable to stop the imprisonment, though I resisted. I assume my uncle turned his attention to my family as well in order to collect as much of their gift and authority as he could."

"Why would he do that?" Usilea fiddled with the pit of her calla orb.

"Because he doesn't have a gift." Larkin's eyes widened. "That's why he had those books on stealing gifts. He must not have one at all."

Petar frowned. "That's quite a leap. It is very rare for any Abstephian to be born without the gift of Making in the smallest amount."

"Perhaps it was so small that he counted it as insignificant," Usilea mused. "People will go to desperate measures to guard themselves when they feel less than others or to repair themselves if they feel broken. My father is an example of that."

She grimaced, the pain deepening in her eyes. Petar wrapped an arm around her shoulders, sharing in her grief. "You are not your father. You are an exceptional queen, and you are mine."

Usilea smiled up at him like sudden sunlight through a storm.

Sunlight ... "We need to move. Now. Once the sun rises, the thornflowers around my family will become far more volatile." He turned to Larkin. "Can you Warp us there?"

"No. It's too ripply." She dropped the plate in her bag. "What he's done in siphoning your magic partly worked. He's somehow stored away a lot of it inside himself. I don't want to risk something awful happening if I Warp us next to him. But he is nearby, so it shouldn't be a far walk."

"Then we must go now."

Without further delay, they set off into the forest. A journey far easier now that Petar was fully aware of himself and his place in Absteph. The mumphlays avoided them, for they had awareness of power through the vitrop. The nal spiders were urged aside with a simple gesture, their webbing undone and drag lines flailing in the cool night breeze. It was the same when Petar had traveled through Braierleve Forest two years ago. At last, the land recognized him fully as one of its stewards and gave him appropriate deference. Even so, he could feel the power rising within himself to potent levels, eager for release.

Usilea tugged at his arm.

"Petar, there are many of the larate pairings here. Even more are behind us."

He turned. The forest floor was filled with the glowing teala fungi and the twinkling purple turqa flowers. A smile touched his lips. "Of course, how could I have forgotten? The vitrop confirms our destined union. It is customary for every fated royal pairing to be acknowledged by them until the day of their full union."

"Oh." Her golden eyes gleamed. "In such number?"

"The number is only in measure to our power and stature. They reflect your gift as well."

Larkin glanced back and raised her eyebrows. "Will they follow you everywhere?"

"I don't know." Petar frowned. "Braierleve is a very old forest, and very strong now."

"Strong because of your power within it?" Usilea tilted her head.

"Yes, because of that."

"Up ahead, you two," Larkin interjected from where she stood at the edge of a new clearing.

If his sense of the land was correct, it was very near where his family was imprisoned—and where Lord Aeson loomed. It must be all of them together. The Making essence emanating from that area was more intense than he had ever felt.

Larkin's voice wavered. "Um, I think Petar should go first."

"Why?" Petar pushed through knee-high brush until he reached where she stood.

"Just that." She flung an arm at the clearing.

His mouth dropped open. Before him rose a large creature of ash and flame. Ropes of vines with enormous leaves and thornflower blossoms covered the great beast, giving it shape and form. Claws made of three-foot-long thorns emerged from each massive paw. A tail swung back and forth, at least four stories in the air.

Usilea rushed up behind him. "What is it? Oh, Eternal help us."

A dragon.

CHAPTER TWELVE

Usilea's blood ran like the cold sea outside of Absteph, and she clenched her hands to stop their trembling. She had heard stories of dragons, fierce creatures who dwelt around fiery mountains. Edrin's mountains were all of solid stone, so they were never at risk, but every so often rumors trickled down from the northern regions.

None of them had mentioned the monstrosity before her. How could it even exist? Surely the plants would be incinerated by the flames or the leaf-like tongue ripped apart by thorn-sharpened teeth.

What could make such a creature?

"I hope you appreciate my work. After all, it came from your power." Lord Aeson sauntered around the side of the dragon, his skin flushed with reddish orange, tinged with brackish green. The colors of passion, anger—and by his aura, bitterness and loathing. His black-and-silver robes flared around him. "There is still time for you to choose more wisely, my queen."

"I am not yours," she spat out. "Nor have I ever been. My betrothed stands with me, and I with him."

She gripped Petar's hand. He squeezed back, then turned and

bent down, his lips close to her ear. "I will face him. Go with Larkin. Free my family. The thornflowers will listen to you if you command them with heart."

Usilea's heart sank. "You've only recently awoken."

"The land is mine, and it will sustain me more than him."

"What if it's wrong?"

"It answers to the Eternal who sees all." He pressed a light kiss to her earlobe, sending a faint tingle through her. "We have fought so hard, my love. This will not part us."

Petar eased back slightly, enough to capture her lips in a brief kiss that teased more. She could barely respond before he moved away.

"No," she breathed.

Grabbing the ripped edges of his open tunic, she pulled him toward her once again for a deeper kiss. Never mind the dragon that roared nearby or the senseless words of Lord Aeson. There was only their lips moving against each other, her fingers daring to trail on the edge of his skin and his fingers tracing the line of her neck.

Alas, breathing was also a necessity, and they parted.

"Don't be foolish, Petar," she gasped. "That is an order."

His mismatched eyes glinted. "As my queen?"

"Yes, and as the woman you vowed you would keep company at night."

Petar took her hands and pressed the backs of them to his own flushed cheeks, then brushed a kiss along the knuckles. "As you wish."

Without another word, he pivoted and strode toward Lord Aeson, his head held high, seemingly at ease despite the fearsome plant dragon.

"I see you have discovered a little of Making, uncle." His tone was dismissive, his skin tinged with oranges and yellows. "Your time torturing me was not ill-spent after all."

"Your Making gift is wasted on you," the false lord sneered. He flung out his arms. The dragon spewed forth more flames aimed directly at Petar.

Usilea's breath froze in her throat.

Her betrothed dodged around the blast and thrust his hands toward the ground. Massive thornflowers sprang up around him, large thorns firing at Lord Aeson.

"A paltry trick." Lord Aeson made a waving gesture. A few large leaves peeled off the plant dragon and shielded him from the missiles. "I would expect that from a frivolous youth."

"Yes, let us enjoy my frivolity," Petar smirked. With another flick of his wrist, a thorn from his flower protectors spun toward his hand. On the way, bark from a nearby tree and a stone from the ground shot up, forming a hilt around the long projectile. "Teach me your wisdom, one who betrays his own family."

Lord Aeson's face twisted. "Your family betrayed everyone when they bartered their most valuable pawn to the enemy."

The dragon swiped a giant clawed foot at Petar.

"You expect to win a bride with those words?" Petar swung the makeshift sword clean through the appendage. The beast roared, filling the air with smoke and the smell of rotten foliage.

Usilea covered her mouth with her sleeve, then whirled around, searching for Larkin. They had to free the rest of the royal family.

A hand grabbed her shoulder. She glanced up to see her friend. Larkin grinned and released her.

"Now *that* is how you kiss. I knew you could do it."

Her cheeks heated. "Um, thanks. This isn't the time. We need to get to Petar's family."

"Warping around the nasty beast?" She squinted at the leather strap with the spinning dials. "The rippling here is even worse, and I'm having trouble sensing those prisons. We might do better running instead."

"I don't run," Usilea hissed.

"You don't?"

"Well, I do, but not especially well. Not now." This night had already left her spent. She sighed. "Please, Larkin."

The Warper ran a hand through her chin-length hair. "What's the point of saving them if you die in the process? That isn't the way to endear myself to the Abstephian prince."

"Larkin!" Usilea's mind searched for something, anything, to change her mind. "Are you saying that you can't accomplish this great feat?"

Her eyes narrowed. "No, not at all. I've opened harder portals."

"Then you're afraid?"

"Never! You might have seen awful things from your parents, but I've dealt with my fair share as well. Afraid." She clicked her teeth. "Goading me? I see your intentions—and I don't care." Yet her hands moved in the air, forcing aside the present realm as though pushing apart two exceptionally heavy doors.

Relief filled Usilea. "You don't care, hm?"

"No, but I also don't want to run right now. Come on, before we die." She grabbed Usilea's hand. "Keep your head together."

Instead of the sensation of a warm bath, the portal scalded her. Boiling water sizzled over every nerve ending, dripping as slowly as lava. When they emerged, she fought the urge to scream. Next to her, Larkin groaned.

"There must be a way around that effect."

"No … time …" Usilea forced the pain aside and fixed her gaze on the thornflower stalks in front of her. Long thorns dripping with deadly toxin burst from every side. The silvery-white petals themselves had barbed edges like wicked saws.

Larkin muttered a harsh word. "Your turn for tricks."

"Your reminder is most kind." Usilea fought to recall what she had done last time. She had knelt on the ground and pressed her blood into the soil. Did she have to repeat that action? Petar had claimed she could command the thornflowers if she had enough heart.

Could the vitrop read such things?

One of the stalks swooped at her, firing several thorns.

"Stones!" She dropped to the ground. Her bones thudded with the impact. "I am not your enemy. I love the man that you serve."

Usilea smacked her palm into the hard-pressed grass, staring into the surface. Trying to see into it, as she did when Mending someone. Reaching out for whatever aura, whatever depths lurked far below. Opening herself to it.

She was met with wariness. The cautious tendrils of a vine testing a new post to grow upon or a shy animal skittish of predators. Was this the vitrop?

So fearful. So very tired, as though the land itself grieved with the loss of its own.

I am here. I know you have suffered. I am familiar with suffering. Usilea allowed herself to fall deeper into the space, letting the vitrop see inside her in turn. *I am here to heal.*

One moment passed, then another.

As slowly as dust motes dancing in a sunbeam.

Glittering. Agonizing.

A quiet sense of peace.

At once, the world around her flickered into sharp focus. Words.

Someone was speaking words.

"—thornflowers are moving! You must go."

Usilea pushed herself to standing. As her friend had spoken, the stalks had parted, forming another archway, their topmost blossoms slightly bent over as they had been earlier.

Acknowledging her as royal. As their ally.

Fresh vigor filled her limbs, and suddenly, running was quite attainable. The still air of the prison met her as she reached the end. A woman lay on the oval platform, her form clad in the black-and-silver robes of Abstephian royalty. The robes made her bleached-white skin even paler. She was near death, as Petar had been.

There was no time to linger.

Usilea bent over, studying the woman's opened eyes. So similar to her son's—was there more life within them? Petar had mentioned that his family might have been taken after he had been, and that he had stood in the gap for them.

She stared into those faintly glittering, pale eyes, letting her forehead rest on the queen's pallid brow.

Seeking for the wounds to Receive. To Mend.

She felt the land reaching out with her, through her, to care for its own. Sharing the heavy burden so that she was not overwhelmed. When the queen's eyes slowly blinked, Usilea was awake and aware enough to move back, albeit clutching the edge of the platform for support.

"You." The words were a hoarse exhalation as the queen rose to her elbows and then to a seated position. "Queen Usilea Searlen. You came to help us."

Usilea nodded. "Yes. Your Majesty, I don't think you should be moving so quickly."

"Why not?" Her light blue eyes crinkled, and her tone was gentle.

"Well, your son was unable to at the start. He pushed himself, and then he needed to rest for a time."

"You found Cowan?" Eagerness filled her voice. Eagerness and a thread of longing.

"I never lost him. We have spoken for years." Steeling herself, Usilea quickly informed Queen Ingard of the events that had transpired, thankful for every bit of poise that had been drilled into her since her childhood.

The queen shook her head, her skin tinting to a pale blue mingled with goldenrod. "That's what he meant when he said that he knew of you already. We didn't have enough time to listen. He had so many other questions, and I was consumed with preparations for his official reunion with our family as one of us." She ran a hand over her dark silver hair. "I often wonder if we were right in that. We had no choice. He was so suspicious of us, so confused. His betrothal to you was the only part that he seemed pleased with."

"He has thought of nothing but protecting you, his people, and the land. He does so even now." Usilea stood, her pulse kicking up. He needed her help.

"As a true member of the royal family should. Unlike my traitorous brother. The land and people come before self." Queen Ingard stood up as well, her skin turning a dark red-brown and her aura radiating grim determination. "Worry not about me. From what I sense through the land, myself, my husband, and my other children have only been trapped here for a year. We will all recover quickly. Come, shall we? The rest of my family will need your gift as well."

She began striding toward the archway, and Usilea sped up to join her. The Abstephian woman had all the confidence of her own mother, yet without a shred of guile. As pure as clear, rushing water.

"In terms of politics, I officially acknowledge you as our son's betrothed and spouse," the queen continued. "The vitrop has already conveyed your value to me in no uncertain terms, and we do not stand on ceremony in Absteph."

Usilea swallowed hard. "Thank you. Your Majesty—"

"Formalities aren't necessary, but we value relations by marriage with honored titles." She turned to face Usilea, her expression softening. "You may call me Lehath, if you wish, and you are Lehathin to me. My husband will be Lehud, and you are Lehudin to him."

"Lehath." The word was strange yet welcoming on her tongue. After years of playing her parents' games of loyalty while planning to betray their wicked schemes, this immediate welcome was odd. It was also odd to have assurance through the vitrop that the queen was true to her word. "If you trust me, then why the delay in contacting me for help? Your son was missing for a year, and we were still betrothed."

They left the confines of the prison. Queen Ingard strode toward another prison of thornflowers a dozen yards away. Larkin jumped to her feet when she saw them approach and walked behind them. Her expression was curiously subdued.

"I trust you now, Lehathin. But then, we were biding our time and watching to see if your legacy would be different from that of your parents. They were known for being as deceitful as a spring rose in winter. After that year, we had decided to send word." Her lips curled. "That was when Aeson revealed his true nature and entrapped us as well. He must face a reckoning."

The firmness with which she said "reckoning" sounded very ... final. "What sort of reckoning?"

"The land will decide."

She halted in front of the next thornflower cluster. At a wave of Queen Ingard's hand, all the stalks bowed down and their thorns retracted. The archway formed instantaneously. She then turned to Usilea.

"Take care that you do not spend all of your reserves on our family. Only revive them, and the land will do the rest, and with greater effect. You are more precious as our daughter-in-law than as a mere healer." She lifted her chin, a smirk on her lips. "As for the Nyarkian who follows us, she will act as a witness. Lady Li-Ann Kwen Throgmorton, are you in a conflict with your Warper houses again?"

"Of a sort." A short laugh echoed from Larkin. "And appreciating your beautiful kingdom, Your Majesty. Also, I have tea and chocolates, and a few new pamphlets on inventions."

The queen gave a wry smile. "As quick-tongued as ever. Well, let us be about it. My brother has done far too much damage to our kingdom. We must made things right."

Chapter Thirteen

His family was awakening. Petar could feel it like a thousand tiny threads of hope and joy, fueling him as he dodged around another blast of flames from the dragon.

Acrid burning rose from the flapping edges of his tunic. His knuckles were seared and throbbing from a close call that almost took out his hands. Above him, the dragon roared and shook his head, the thorn-like horns gleaming in the early daylight, the frills of curled leaves and molten embers of rock quivering with outrage.

Not only outrage. Fear. Through the vitrop, Petar could sense waves of fear and confusion emanating from the beast as it lunged at him once more under the authority of Lord Aeson. He would never call him uncle again.

The enemy scowled at him from his position behind and to the left of the dragon. "You were always too stubborn for your own good, Cowan. Clinging to an abundance of power that cannot benefit you or your people."

"It is not for you to steal that power." He brought up the flat of his blade, deflecting the dragon's attack with one swing and slicing into his broadside with another.

It was not a deep slice. It would be a pity to kill such a magnificent creation. Lord Aeson might have used his knowledge and stolen Maker gifts to manifest the beast, but the vitrop and the Eternal had to permit such an act. That meant the plant dragon was neutral. Perhaps it could be saved, tamed so that it would wander Braierleve, at home with the other dangers within the forest.

After all, the power had been stolen from him for years.

Could he use it to gain mastery of the dragon?

Lord Aeson stalked closer, his own blade at the ready. Did he sense Petar's intention? "Not the Eternal, nor any of our gods of old, can command me."

"Then how is it that a youth withstood you for two years?"

"You frost-cursed mumphlay!" The traitor charged at him with his sword through the dragon's forelegs, his face a mask of fury and anger, skin tinted orange and blood-red. Flames from the beast ate away at the lengths of his robes.

Petar dropped to the ground in a crouch, hands pressing into the scuffed soil and grass. The vitrop met his demand. He rolled to the side just as walls of rock rose from the ground five feet. Ten feet. Twenty.

Waves of power crashed against the rocks, but they held firm. As they should have, for the power was his own. Was Lord Aeson so arrogant that he believed Petar wouldn't fight back?

Disgust roiled within him. The man had expected Usilea to abandon her kingdom, responsibilities, and throne for his esteemed wit and wisdom. So she had told Petar during their journey through Braierleve earlier. It was clear as winter ice that the man was indeed delusional.

Let him be so. Petar needed every advantage in this maneuver.

He had taken control of small manifestations created by his siblings, mostly as a prank, but never one of this magnitude, a beast of myth and legend. Never had he stolen a dragon.

But it was the only way to save it.

Rising to a half-bent position, Petar ran as fast as he dared around the clearing, drawing up more and more walls of rock to deflect attacks. Such a feat should have left him spent and near collapse, but the vitrop allowed him to do so easily, as though he were merely raising up grass. More power rose within him, ready to do whatever he bid.

Soon the dragon and Lord Aeson were surrounded by the high stone walls, although the dragon still loomed above them. Petar stood to his full height on the other side of the clearing. The beast whirled around to face him once more, its dark red eyes glowing softly.

Filled with pain as much as with ferocity.

What a beautiful, inexplicable creation, made of fiery coals and heat from the distant mountains and fresh leaves from the trees of Braierleve. Trees that Petar himself had helped to revive. For he could weave the impossible together. He had to, in order to relieve the burden of his gift.

Petar reached out a hand toward the dragon, allowing his Making to extend through the land into the creature.

"Come now. You don't want to hurt me."

The tip of the plant dragon's tail twitched back and forth above the rock, and its leafy ears flicked on the top of its head.

"Easy. Listen to my voice. I don't wish to harm you either. It would be better if both of us could roam freely, wouldn't it now?"

He heard thorn-claws scrape at the ground, but otherwise, the plant dragon remained still. Watchful. Attuning to his voice.

"What are you doing, nephew?" Lord Aeson's exclamation broke through his focus. "You dare to think you can claim my creation?"

The rock walls shook. Petar forced every part of his body to remain calm and relaxed. He needed the dragon to trust him, to understand that he was in command.

He reached out through the vitrop to the dragon, sensing every thornflower, every coal, every twist of vine and scrap of bark that composed it. A discordant composition, for Lord Aeson only thought of brute strength to enable his attacks, not of how to truly construct a creature who would be aligned with the world around it.

"Listen to me." He hummed the words, never breaking eye contact with the dragon. Not forcing the power, only gently reminding it of to whom it rightfully belonged. Welcoming the power and the plant dragon back to their true home. "I will make you well, as you were meant to be."

For he would sooner destroy the finest painting than the creature before him. The Eternal had allowed it to exist. Petar's duty was to see that it thrived. Free.

The beast tilted his head, then took a step toward him.

"I demand you stop!"

The rock wall shuddered again as Lord Aeson brought all of his remaining strength destroy to the barrier. Alarm shot through Petar. His mind could not create any other obstacles, not with the dragon so keenly in need of his help.

Dust and pebbles broke from the wall, clattering on the ground.

His heart pounded in his ears.

The vitrop flowed between him and the dragon, weaving together like to like, need to caregiver. The dragon gave a low stream of steam and flames that curled around Petar as a light embrace, floating inches from his skin and clothing but not harming him.

He could spare nothing for Lord Aeson's taunts. Not even a glance in his direction.

"As I thought. You bear the same weakness as the rest of your family." The wall fell to the ground, and he crunched across it. "Needlessly enamored of the creation to your own detriment." Disdain shredded Lord Aeson's voice. "Now you will die—"

His voice cut off into a strangled choke. Out of the corner of his eye, Petar saw that thick thornflower stalks pressed in around the traitor and vines encircled his throat tightly.

"This land has suffered enough of your lies, Lord Aeson," a deep, resonant voice boomed across the clearing, the tones sinking within Petar's heart. "It is time you were silenced."

His father. King Andryn.

The plant dragon roared an agreement, slamming its foreleg into the ground. The firmament shook through Petar, and Lord Aeson fell unconscious.

"Let the land that you have misused decide your fate," the king continued. "Let there be a reckoning of the vitrop before the family you betrayed and the Eternal who sees all."

The air seemed to shimmer with power and intensity, like the space near the edges of a fierce fire.

A peal of thunder vibrated through the quiet. The ground shook once more, then shivered apart, revealing a chasm directly below Lord Aeson. Flames licked up at his prone form, devouring the vines and stalks until there was nothing more suspending him and he fell into the depths.

Another clap of thunder, a rustling, crackling sound as the soil reformed.

Then there was nothing except a circular symbol of scorch marks and jagged lettering. The mark of a decided for any who needed proof.

Petar exhaled slowly.

The land had decided.

A high, sibilant groan broke through his sudden weariness. Through the vitrop, he felt the pain jolting through the dragon's foreleg. Pain from the wound he had inflicted.

"Easy now. Be still." With a simple request, new foliage sprang up from the ground to wrap around the foot and foreleg.

"A true son of mine."

He turned toward his father's voice. A relation through the vitrop and through a handful of interactions and distant acknowledgements. Now King Andryn's face, wreathed by a long, white-blond beard, shone with the soft golden-pink of family affection.

Petar cleared his throat and brushed a bit of grass off what remained of his tunic. "I only did as anyone would have done."

A woman with a braided crown of dark silver hair and a kind, firm expression stood beside King Andryn. His mother, Queen Ingard. "No, you have not. Observe the sad symbol of your departed uncle."

"I would rather look upon my betrothed." He searched behind them. Two more figures walked forward. Fria with her long braid of white-blonde hair and Raffer's broad, armor-covered chest came into view. Between them, they supported a shorter, more delicate figure with disheveled black hair and weary steps.

His heart caught in his throat.

"Usilea?"

"I am well." Her head slowly inclined upward to meet his stare, her golden eyes crinkling with weariness and her chin managing a defiant tilt. "Or at least, I shall be soon. I'm not used to much Receiving."

Indeed, she had only done it a scant number of times during the past few years. Before he could think, he was moving toward her, eager to take her in his arms. She had given far more than anyone could expect.

Behind him, the plant dragon gave a plaintive cry.

Queen Ingard raised her hand, her silver-and-black sleeve swaying gently in the breeze. "Mind the creature, my son. Your siblings are managing the welfare of their new sister."

"You accept her so easily?"

Now King Andryn looked upon Petar as well, his skin turning pale blue and violet, shades of surprise. "Why would we not? She has more than proven her worth and loyalty to the family. The land accepts her." His voice softened a fraction. "Why would we not?"

He was grateful. Their acceptance of his beloved was welcome. And yet …

You sent me away. Petar clenched his jaw to avoid speaking the words. They were unkind. Unfair, perhaps. His family had done what they thought was best by hiding him and raising him in obscurity. No one could capture him. Braierleve had contained his excess of power and given him a place to turn his gift into healing a hopeless forest. He had been raised carefree, knowledgeable of his people but without the deep traditions of a royal. He was powerful enough to live in another country and only return a handful of times a year without it affecting his gift.

Still, his chest tightened. The last few years, he had only thought of resistance, of guarding his family and land as an instinctive, right act. There was nothing left to say.

The king exchanged a look with the queen, then strode more quickly to Petar. He couldn't read his father's expression—or perhaps, didn't want to. Instead, Petar turned toward where the dragon beckoned for his attentions. The beast's eager expression brought a smile to his lips despite the chaotic emotions whirling within him.

"Very good." He gave a clicking sound. "What do you need? A morsel of food?"

"You will have to discover this." The king was near enough to radiate warmth in the cool morning air. A large, square hand settled on Petar's shoulder. "You have done well to take mastery of him through compassion and understanding."

He nodded, shifting a little under the compliment. "My guardians taught me well. They died when I was attacked. Lord Aeson took great pleasure in informing me of this as well as how he had disguised the nature of his attacks."

"They had honorable deaths. We gave them suitable funerals." The king cleared his throat. "I wish it had been me who had taught you instead. Your mother and I made the best choice for the kingdom and for you, not for ourselves."

"So you said earlier." The words fell out like flat stones, even as the plant dragon craned its neck toward him and nudged his hand. "The greatest weight of our roles is that unlike our people, we must honor others and the land before our family. In this, we are an example to our people, and in this we serve them."

The statements were colder than the air around them. He knew them well. It didn't ease his discomfort now. Was there anything he could say that would somehow build goodwill?

Petar stroked the plant dragon's nose, searching his sleep-addled mind.

"I will be leaving soon for Edrin with my queen, so your actions were wise."

"Yes, I see that they were."

He shifted from one foot to another. "This dragon will need

new companions. I'm … unsure of how to move its allegiance from me to others."

"It will always carry some allegiance to you." King Andryn's words came more easily, as though with a thread of excitement. "But it can be attuned to the rest of your family as well. It will acknowledge those whom you acknowledge and those whom you trust."

Petar turned his head to give his father a brief glance, letting his own face reveal more of his feelings. Caution, curiosity. Fragile hope. "We can both learn to trust."

The king squeezed his shoulder. "I would like that. Very much."

"Then, if you are both settled, Lady Larkin has opened a portal." His mother's voice was brisk but undergirded with warmth. "Also, there is a wedding to plan, for my son will not leave his homeland without a proper ceremony."

"Aye! Come, take your bride, brother," Raffer called out. "For such a small one, she grows heavy for our arms."

Petar grinned. "She is perfect."

"Carry your perfect queen, then."

With suddenly light steps, he ran toward his betrothed.

CHAPTER FOURTEEN

"Mind your step, Lehathin."

Usilea glanced down at her shoes. Just below her uplifted foot were turqa flowers and teala fungi. The larate pairing, symbolizing a destined royal pairing.

She sighed imperceptibly and moved her foot to the side, adjusting her position on the cushioned stone bench where she sat next to Queen Ingard.

"I'm sorry." She did her best to keep her voice sweet and polite. Never mind that at this point she wanted to stomp on the dreadful things. They had become less magical the more they had invaded any outside excursion. "Are they behind me as well?"

"They are indeed." Queen Ingard gave a small chuckle. "I imagine you're ready to be married at this point."

Usilea stole a glance at her future mother-in-law. Her words were calm and understated, but her skin was soft yellow mixed with a tinge of green. Amusement and shared irritation, confirmed by her aura.

"I am finding that it would be convenient for a number of

reasons, Lehath."

The queen studied her for a moment. Petar had mentioned that Abstephians found it difficult to read outsiders due to the lack of skin color changes. Usilea did her best to show affection and a bit of irritation on her face, and she allowed her emotions to filter into the vitrop as well. After a moment, Queen Ingard chuckled again and gave her shoulder a single, light pat.

"Yes, it will be. It will also be far easier on the gardeners." She relaxed, adjusting her deep red cotehardie and dark brown cloak, both garments edged with velvet and intricately stitched with patterns and quilting. Unlike the Reign Lord, Queen Ingard seemed secure enough not to wear her country's official colors every moment of the day. "Are there any questions you have before the ceremony tomorrow morning?"

Usilea studied the stone table in front of them which held the remains of their early afternoon meal. It had been filled with rich cheeses and bread as well as smoked meats and artfully sliced fish. Unlike the queen's hearty appetite, her own portions had been small. The meal had included conversations over trade possibilities and new partnerships. It was challenging to eat much when considering the future and trying to navigate the best possible deals while building positive relationships.

"Is it typical for destined pairs to speak with thoughts?"

Her future mother-in-law nodded. "Yes, especially as they grow closer and fonder of each other. The bond continues after the marriage and is anchored in the vitrop."

This aligned with what Usilea had seen between the queen and king. After their initial reunion, they had quickly taken to their private mental conversations. The rapid changing of their skin tones and shifts in aura revealed it, although she didn't observe too closely to avoid being rude. Besides, some information she didn't want to know.

Anchored in the vitrop. Isn't that interesting, Petar?

No reply. Only silence, just as it had been in the days since she, Petar, and the royal family had returned to the Willowing Halls.

She hid another sigh. What was she doing wrong?

"Thank you, Lehath. I have enjoyed our conversation. I think I will take some time for solitude."

"Naturally." Queen Ingard smiled in understanding. Abstephians seemed to have a strong appreciation for quiet reflection. "Lehathin, trust in the Eternal. Your bond will settle down."

"Thank you. I will try." Usilea exchanged leavetakings with her, then rose and walked to her room. She kept her pace light and quick to avoid the larate pairing and reached out to the vitrop. Maybe she simply wasn't trying hard enough?

At her lightest probe, the shivery sort of awareness trickled in. Her lips curved at the contact. Again, she tried to reach out to Petar. *Are you there, my prince?*

No response. Not even a hint of teasing emotion or a flicker of love.

Eternal, please make a way for us to hear each other again.

Petar seemed to think it would work out. He tended to be more optimistic than her.

At last, Usilea lay curled up in blankets in her room with a cup of hot herb broth and a palace cat with black fur and golden eyes at her feet. The last night she would sleep alone. On that matter, she felt absolute security and, yes, eagerness to begin her life with Petar after so many years connecting through their strange bond.

A connection that itself was now … different. Altered somehow, in ways she couldn't quite define except—

The shimmer of air around the foot of her bed made Usilea sit up, clutching the earthenware mug with one hand. The other reached for a small knife underneath her pillow.

"Larkin?"

The air tore in two, then the familiar figure stepped through. This time she wore a brown-and-blue striped dress that fell to delicate boots and was cinched about the waist with a black corset. The neckline closed around her chin with a frill of lace, and her black hair was pinned back into small loops and soft waves.

"Oh, Larkin ..."

"Go ahead, laugh." She gave a sardonic smile. "Everyone does when I'm wearing this kind of clothing."

Usilea shook her head, but she couldn't repress the curve of her lips. "I'm simply unused to it. You look lovely."

"Sure I do." At that moment, Usilea realized her friend was carrying a tray with small pastries and shortbread, as well as four glasses. Two were large and filled with a white liquid. The other two were small and the contents were clear, warm brown. "You wouldn't have seen me in this fussy rig except that I decided to stop by the kitchen and commandeer some sustenance for us instead of changing in my room."

She walked over, set the tray on the edge of the bed, and sat down beside it. Then she nimbly rolled up her long sleeves, leaned down, unlaced the boots, and kicked them off.

"Ah, much better. Now, a toast?" Larkin gestured to the brown glasses. "It's not traditional to toast with cusk liquor, but I could use a shot to settle my nerves."

Usilea shook her head. "No, thank you. Pass me the milk—for it is milk, yes? Only milk?"

"Only milk." Her friend handed her the drink. "Is strong drink not allowed for you? I thought you were eighteen, like me."

"I am, but there *will* be traditional toasts at the wedding ceremony. I can wait until then." It wouldn't be wise to let herself indulge now. She would be representing her kingdom and taking vows before the Eternal.

"I, on the other hand, cannot wait." Larkin shrugged and tipped back the shot. "To not waiting." She reached for the other glass.

Usilea cleared her throat. "So, what of your troubles?"

The Nyarkian's hand paused on its journey. Instead, she grabbed a glazed spiral roll stuffed with nuts. "My father is ill, and I can't tell anyone. Except for you. I trust that after all of this, you can keep a secret."

"Of course!" Usilea hastily swallowed her milk. "That's terrible. How long has your father been ill?"

"It's complicated." Larkin eyed the shot again. Then she sighed and closed her eyes, pinching the bridge of her nose. "Do you know if your Mending works on hereditary illnesses?"

"Ones passed down through a bloodline? It depends on the type. I would have to do some research once I return home to Edrin—or ask Priest Valtor and Renna to do the research." Usilea pressed her lips together. "My official coronation will take place when I return, which means even more responsibilities."

Her friend grinned suddenly. "Many congratulations! You'll be an excellent official queen."

"Thank you." Usilea nibbled on one of the shortbreads. "Can you tell me anything about your father's illness? I would like to help. You've done so much for Petar and me over these past few days."

"I don't know if you can." Larkin scuffed her fingernails on the coverlet. "I mentioned when we first met that I was growing tired of funerals. That's because a lot of Warpers in Nyark are ... sick. It's their own fault, I say. The houses like to keep the bloodlines pure, and that can make those families small and marriages very close at hand." She shook her head and suddenly her words spilled out much faster. "Inbreeding, in other words. It caused a sickness—the Strand—that makes Warpers who use their gift get weak and sort of come apart at the seams until eventually they disintegrate entirely into the essence and beyond."

Usilea fell silent for a moment. She didn't want to imply anything, but if she were to help, she needed to know. "Your father has this sickness?"

"No! That's what makes it so strange. He couldn't have had it. My parents are from very different houses from different lands. It's one of the reasons I'm so valuable as a marriage partner. I must have many children to improve the line and grow the houses." Larkin finished off another nut roll. "Which would have been easier if my betrothed, Lord Virgil, had not sent me a writ of separation."

"What?" Usilea set down her glass of milk. "He called off the arranged marriage?"

"Yes, with a letter penned by his servant. He couldn't even write it with his own hand."

"What was the reason?"

"None was given." Her jaw worked, and she swiped at her eyes. "I shouldn't be surprised. He has been distant for months, but … he seemed certain about our marriage before that. I don't understand."

Usilea nodded sympathetically. "What will you do?"

She exhaled a shuddery breath. "My father is ill. I must focus on finding the cure to save him and preserve the name and honor of the Houses Kwen and Throgmorton. Which is why I asked if you knew about curing hereditary illnesses caused by inbreeding that could not have occurred."

"That does sound very difficult. Without knowing more, there isn't much I can do. But I don't think another swallow of strong drink is the answer."

Larkin rolled her eyes. "It would make me forget about it all for a bit."

"Even so." Usilea reached out hesitantly and squeezed her hand. "I'm sure there's something you can figure out. You're clever enough."

"Maybe. If it comes to the worst, I can always elope with some beastly shut-in who has a lot of books and an excessive amount of arcane knowledge. Perhaps we can come up with something to heal Father."

"Yes, that's precisely what I was thinking." Usilea tsked.

Larkin flashed a grin, seemingly eager to forget her troubles. The gears at the edges of her eyes winked in the light. "So why are you brooding in here? Shouldn't you be sneaking some time with your betrothed before the ceremony?"

"I suppose." She wrinkled her nose and focused on the milk in her glass.

"Not having second thoughts, are you?"

"No!" Usilea grabbed a pillow and lightly swatted her friend with it. "Never."

The Nyarkian chuckled. "Good. I had an awful headache after making all those complex portals in one night. So, why are you hiding?"

"I'm not hiding. I'm thinking."

"About what?"

She pressed her lips together and offered the black cat a taste of her milk. Was it a foolish thing to admit? Still, Larkin had shared her own problems.

"I'm ... afraid."

"Afraid of what?"

"I'm not sure. I just … our entire lives, we've been able to hear each other." She ran her finger along the edge of the empty glass. "I can't hear Petar in my head anymore. It's very … lonely."

"Have you talked with him about it?"

Usilea burrowed deeper under the covers. "Well, a little, but there have been a lot of details to sort out with the ceremony, and he's been busy trying to connect with his family before he has to leave, and—it's harder when I have to speak it aloud!"

A pillow sailed in her direction. She squeaked and dodged it.

"You've already confessed your love to him. Use more of that boldness." Larkin smirked. "If it goes poorly, kiss him again. It's a good way to end a conversation that isn't going well." Her lips turned downward. "Unless he tries to talk while you're kissing him. Lord Virgil tended to do that, which was rather adorable, the way his eyes would—" She gave her shoulders a shake. "Really, a hermit with some sort of deformity might be what I need. Enough with handsome lords. Right now, if a man was rational, and kind-hearted, and listened. If he didn't just disappear. Yes, that would be good." The Warper paused, her gaze turning distant. "Wait a moment. I wonder…"

Usilea cleared her throat. "You aren't helping yourself or me, my friend."

Larkin gave her a gentle shove. "Then help yourself like the queen that you are."

She eyed Larkin. "Are you all right?"

"Oh, I have an idea." Her jaw worked. "I might know exactly how, and where, to find Virgil."

Usilea frowned. "Don't you want to forget about him and care for your father?"

"Yes. I also want to confront my former betrothed and learn

why he changed from devotion to rejecting me. If I'm clever, as you say, I can do that while helping my father and finding the hermit." Larkin smiled, then she turned to Usilea. "Speaking of which, go find your prince. And don't worry. If you find yourself distracted, between your guards and me, we can get you ready for the ceremony very fast." She winked.

"I won't be that long." Eternal forbid she be late to her own wedding.

"Good, because this lovely lady here and I are going to scheme." Larkin stroked the cat's back, then coaxed her over with a bit of savory pastry. "And then after your wedding, I have to hire a Hunter for my quest."

"Very well."

Emerging from the covers, Usilea found her gown wrinkled. She took Larkin's advice to wear a cloak over top. A quick touch into the vitrop revealed that Petar stood in the broad green field in front of the Willowing Halls.

Which meant he was with the dragon.

A thrill of excitement shot through Usilea as she slipped through the palace and into the cool evening air, her guards at her side. The ceremony would take place at the first light of dawn on that lawn, when the thornflowers were brightest to honor the event. Right now, the blossoms were closed tightly, though their gleaming silver-white petals were still beautiful.

As she walked across the grass, she beheld another incredible sight. Her betrothed stood before the plant dragon, petting its snout. Bittersweet joy filled her. The dragon seemed so content, its leaves floating gently around in the breeze and the coals within burning brightly.

Who am I to take that away from him? Her heart clenched with the thought, a musing she had tried so hard to repress. She motioned for her guards to remain at a distance so as not to alarm the beast.

Petar turned toward her, and a bright smile lit up his face, which tinted yellow-orange with happiness. He waved at her in what was clearly a beckoning gesture. But there were no words in her mind, only his expression. Was that lost in the past they had shared? Did he even want to leave this place?

He would. For her, Petar would do anything. Also, he had to leave for the safety of his country. The land was reviving under the care of the royal family, but the king had warned it would soon be overwhelmed with Petar's power once again.

"I'm glad you've come," he said when she drew close enough to hear him. "Over two weeks, and I still don't have a name for him. Father says the vitrop will guide me, but we leave the day after the wedding, and nothing has been revealed. I was hoping you could help."

"I don't know many Abstephian names suitable for animals."

"Thankfully, that is not a requirement for our marriage." Petar pulled her into a hug, which she returned fiercely. Stones, but he smelled so good. Some undefinable fresh woodsy scent, as though Braierleve always clung to him. At last they parted, and he pressed a kiss to the tip of her nose.

"It doesn't have to be an Abstephian name," he continued, his eyes shining. "I thought if the land wouldn't give me the name, then maybe it would give us the name if we asked together."

She swallowed, trailing her fingertip absently over his chest, clad in a whole black tunic layered with a deep blue cloak. An outfit which was far more appropriate than his ripped clothing, even if a part of her fondly remembered when his skin had been bare. "I would like that. Only ..."

"Only what?"

"Only I don't hear *you*. That is difficult to bear."

Oh no, what had she done? Had she spoken those words aloud? It was far easier when he could just be within her mind.

At least they were out now, no matter what catastrophe happened next.

Petar tilted his head, emotions flickering over his face. "My parents told me we should trust the vitrop and the Eternal."

"I've tried, but … I miss you." Her fingers stopped their wandering, her palm flattening against his sternum. "I miss us. I feel as though I'm missing a piece of myself, and it is so odd to be coming upon our wedding morning …"

"Grieving," he whispered, gently cupping her face with his long fingers. "You are not alone in this, goldenbird. Though when you spoke of being content, I tried to be as well."

"You aren't?"

His mouth cut a thin line. "No. You're part of my soul, and this separation is agonizing."

She stared up at him. "Then what are we to do now?"

"I might have an idea."

"You've had an idea this entire time and didn't tell me?" Usilea did her best to glare at him. It was hard when his face was bright with new thoughts that she desperately wanted to hear.

"It only came to me just now." Petar moved away from her and toward the dragon. "You say you've heard the land, but I can't sense you through the vitrop. Nor can my family. We know you are accepted and linked, but we cannot sense you as we would expect."

She bit her lip, walking toward the dragon as well. It inclined its head toward her, whuffling softly. Likely eager for dry, dead roots. For a plant dragon, the beast had the appetite of a carnivore and preferred wood to feed the fire within.

Usilea held out her hands. "I'm sorry. I didn't bring anything with me."

"Goldenbird? Do you truly sense the land?"

"I do, only … I don't know what to do." She searched for more words. "I've had to rely on myself for so long that to have another presence seems … intrusive. Other than yours."

His face softened. "I understand. It has been odd to become reacquainted with my family. I do what I can because I want to love them, and I do, but—"

"They sent you away."

"It is much to overlook." He gestured her closer, then knelt on the ground. Usilea crouched beside him, settling her skirt and the cloak around her. "Our own bond might be woven with the land, which means only with the land could we find it again. This dragon might be part of that."

"Part of that, how?"

"I don't know. That was the extent of my idea." Petar took her hand in his. "I'm willing to try, if you are."

Usilea knew what he was asking. To open herself to the vitrop. Not to beg for assistance, but simply to be vulnerable with the land, and in doing so, connect with those who lived on it. Would they accept her? How much would they know of what she had seen, of what she had had to do?

Although, the royal family had accepted the loss of their own traitorous brother at the reckoning. Surely they would understand her subterfuge for the greater good. How she had to keep secrets even from her own brother in order to orchestrate the overthrow.

She felt Petar's gaze on her. Not impatient, simply waiting. Intimately familiar with her need to think deeply before acting.

One deep breath, then exhale.

"I am willing."

"My brave, beautiful queen." He pressed a gentle kiss to the back of her hand, then placed it on the ground with his own atop it.

"What must I do?"

"Ask for the name of the dragon. The vitrop isn't a being as you or I am. It needs guidance to guide you in turn."

Usilea shut her eyes tightly and pushed into the grass, setting her jaw.

Her betrothed's chuckle broke through her concentration. "Grip and grind goes the stone below the depths of the highest ocean and coldest flame."

"No nonsense. I am trying to focus, my lord."

"Yes, I can see that and almost hear your teeth clenching. The vitrop doesn't seek your harm. You don't need to brace yourself." His fingers stroked the back of her hand, drawing small threads of warmth. "You are safe here, my queen of starlight."

"All right." Usilea sighed, letting her shoulders relax.

She sensed the curious rhythms of the land beneath her, attentive in a way that brought to mind Opal. Slowly, she opened herself to that attention, letting her own nervousness escape, her own uncertainty about what to do with this immense force. Her desire for that bond with her betrothed and for the name of the dragon.

A feeling that could only be described as friendliness flowed through her. Not pushing her or judging her. It was as though the vitrop was coiling around her legs with the ownership of a cat. Loyal, but also independent, understanding that she would leave soon, and so would Petar. But they would return?

She sent reassurance into the land. They would return.

Contentment like a pleasantly flowing stream eased her mind and unknotted the tight bundles of thoughts she picked at ceaselessly.

Amund.

Yes, the plant dragon's name was Amund.

Amund.

"A good name." The voice in her mind crackled with familiarity. Not her own, but as near as her own heartbeat.

Petar? Her eyes opened and stared into his.

"I told you it need not be painful."

As elation filled her like the purest rays of sunlight, Usilea realized that Larkin was right. Sometimes the only answer to a smug reply was a firm kiss that he quickly responded to. Then a second kiss, deep and full of joy. And another, wrapping her arms around him and running her fingers through his hair as he stroked up and down her back. She savored his taste, their shared fervor and heat, minds once more united.

Thank the Eternal. She had missed him so much.

An excited, squealing sound finally broke through the haze and convinced them to part, if only briefly.

Usilea stared up at the dragon, who almost seemed to be prancing as though he anticipated something unexpectedly marvelous.

The answer came a moment later through the vitrop.

She turned to Petar, trying to catch up with this sudden change.

Will Amund survive apart from the land?

"It would appear so. The vitrop seems to have bound him with us and our giftings."

Usilea raised her eyebrows. *Did you plan this?*

"Would I ever?"

At the glint in his eyes, she couldn't help but grin.

The journey home had suddenly become far more complicated.

Chapter Fifteen

It's so warm down here. Petar hid the thought from his wife, only because she had heard it three times already, as their flotilla sailed the last few miles to the shoreline of Edrin. He had wondered at first when Usilea had suggested lighter clothing, but now he understood. Even with the fine tunic and trousers with thin boots, he was sweating.

Although that could also be due to the upcoming meeting with his new relatives who would be waiting for them at the dock. He inhaled a mild, salty breeze then exhaled slowly, continuing his pacing up and down the length of the ship and giving quick smiles to the crew members he accidentally bumped into. They were used to his meanderings by now.

Reaching the end of the ship, he stared behind him at the other two vessels. One held a small delegation from Absteph, including his brother Raffer, to witness their wedding ceremony in Edrin as well as Usilea's coronation ceremony. The third ship was mostly occupied by Amund. The first creature created by Abstephian Makers to leave their shores.

At this moment, Amund was crouched on top of his ship, taking up the entire middle deck, his tail winding around the poop deck and his head craning around the masts in the forecastle. His dark red eyes flickered with flames as he observed the surroundings.

I understand, my friend. He sent the plant dragon a pulse of reassurance through their bond. A bond that Usilea also shared. With a nudge, the plant dragon made his way below deck via the large doors cut into one side of the top deck. The people of Edrin would need to be carefully introduced to their new friend and ally. *I'm glad you're here with me.*

"*As am I.*" His beloved's voice trickled into his mind. After they had married and known each other even more, the link had grown stronger and clearer. Another comfort as he left his homeland. He could feel her amusement. "*My brother knows of you, but I haven't told him of Amund. Jaric needs a few surprises to make sure he doesn't grow complacent as a father.*"

Petar grinned. *Ironic, considering your own love of surprises.*

"*I merely want to share my wonderful fortune with others. Come, we're about to enter the bay.*"

"Your Majesty, your presence is requested by the queen on the main deck." The first mate gave him a respectful nod and a half-bow, his silver-tinted olive skin gleaming in the morning sun.

"Thank you, Nunor. You, the captain, and the entire crew have done an excellent job." He smiled, focusing to make sure his face and hands were only lightly tinged with pale bluish-gray. The Edrinians were still growing accustomed to the changing tones.

"A pleasure, sir. You're a welcome presence aboard ship. Thank you for the gift for my daughter."

"A small token. I hope she enjoys it."

"That she will. Have a good morn." Nunor's lips quirked in

an answering smile before striding off. An Abstephian would have simply bowed and left quietly with no conversation. The outgoing nature of the ship's crew was a fair introduction to the different life he would be leading. Given how hard it was to read them, Petar was grateful for the openness in other areas and had tried his best to reciprocate. At least in that regard, his innate sensibilities were an asset. In Absteph, he had always been known as extraordinarily talkative.

"If you are finished flattering the crew, I would appreciate you by my side." Fresh humor colored Usilea's voice.

I am merely making friends. I like friends. He moved down to the main deck where she stood, wearing a vibrant blue-and-gold traveling dress that left her arms bare and brought out the garnet accents in her deep brown skin. *Have I mentioned how glorious you look?*

Her golden eyes glowed and her lips curved. *"That flattery I will accept."*

It isn't flattery, only honesty. Petar kissed the back of her neck where her hair was gathered into a knot and set off by the simple circlet of interwoven gold in her hair. *If you would prefer me to stop—*

"No. That's all right." She turned to face him, adjusting the fit of the dark blue tunic over his shoulders, her fingers lingering on his chest. *"I'm quite pleased with you myself. I've always been uncomfortable with the expectation of affectionate displays among my people. You make it far easier."*

I'm happy to serve, as always. His fingers caressed her upper back.

She pressed her lips together, her eyes crinkling. *"You do well."*

A high, fluting trumpet sounded. "Her Majesty's ship *The Seaspoken* has arrived. Make ready for Their Majesties to offboard!"

They parted, but continued holding hands. Petar stared out over the shore. A large city clustered along the coastland, its stone buildings featuring bright colors and patterned tiles. The buildings crowded steeply into the hillside with narrow streets tangled between, and most of the streets were filled with people.

So different from Absteph.

Usilea squeezed his hand. *"You are mine, and I am yours. We will do fine."*

Eternal help them, they would. They had found each other and fought for each other. This would be a new adventure.

They descended the stairway that had been secured to the edge of the ship. As soon as Petar stepped onto the land, a bit of his tension released. The land slept here, but it carried the same essence that supported gifts. He would grow used to the difference and learn to understand Edrin for its own beauty.

He turned to a young man with broad shoulders, a square-jawed face, and dark brown hair that was neatly trimmed. He wore black trousers and a dark blue tunic similar to Petar's, but with a black coat over it with an insignia on the right panel. At the moment, a baby held in his arms seemed to be doing its best to pry off that insignia. This had to be Usilea's brother and former regent, Prince Jaricob Searlen. The silver, woven circlet set him apart, as did his skin, garnet-touched like hers but a few shades lighter.

Next to him stood a woman over a head shorter with loose, dark hair that reached past her shoulders, deep cobalt eyes, and silver-toned olive skin. She wore a dark brown-and-red dress with a white cloak and held another baby who seemed to be sleeping. The prince's wife, Princess Corenne Searlen, who was also a leader of the Mender sanctuary along with her father.

"Jaric! It's good to see you." Usilea ran up to her brother and flung her arms around his neck, heedless of the baby. Then she stepped back with a grin. "I see that Jarry is still attached to you."

His sober expression melted into a half-smile. "Yes, apparently he's eager to sign up for military service, despite my warnings."

"He listens as well as his father, then."

"Indeed," Princess Corenne put in with a mischievous look. "Although Jarry has many years to change his mind." She hugged Usilea as well, then her glance traveled to Petar. Her face shifted to what might have been understanding. "And is this your betrothed, Prince Cowan of Absteph?"

Usilea turned toward him and gestured him forward. "Yes. Well, he's my husband now. Petar, this is Jaric and Renna."

He stepped up next to her, smiling broadly. "Also, I prefer to be called Petar by friends and family. I am Cowan only in formal scenarios or when others are angry at me."

"Well, Cowan, how is it that you're married to my sister before her ceremony in her own country?" Jaric's green eyes were hard.

A challenge? Very well. He could oblige.

"My parents insisted," he answered mildly. "After all, they wanted the opportunity to celebrate our union among my people and in our land. They were unable to join us due to the current political upheaval."

"You do seem far less dead than messages conveyed."

Usilea shoved him. "Jaric, stop it. I sent word as soon as we rescued his family. You knew of our wedding as well. At least I didn't try to run away from my country and responsibilities."

"I was advancing in a better direction." His lips twitched.

"Liar." She shrugged. "Besides, I required his presence in my cabin on the return voyage. It wouldn't have been appropriate without a ceremony."

At that, Jaric gave a short laugh. "I've been in your cabin on voyages. I've held back your hair while you leaned over a basin. Very romantic for your wedding night."

Petar cleared his throat. "That took place before we embarked."

A daring remark, perhaps, but it was odd simply standing there while his brother-in-law judged him. Usilea had warned him that in Edrin there wasn't the same immediate acceptance of married family as there was in Absteph. Still, Jaric's response seemed especially cold.

"Did it?" The prince gave him another measuring stare. "And you think I should know this, Cowan?"

"Well, we are brothers now. According to Usilea, it was a surprise to the entire palace that you and your wife were not expecting soon after the wedding day."

Renna gave a small giggle, her cheeks flushing. For his part, Jaric paused for a second. Then he smirked.

"Here, brother, take your nephew." He held out the baby. "If you drop him, I have a reason to kill you."

"What if he likes me more than you?" Petar received the squirming child, who immediately began crying.

"Then I will finally have a chance to sleep."

He pulled out a small stick and a rock from his pocket with his free hand and held them out before little Jarry. Then, drawing upon the power of the sleeping land, Petar caused the two objects to merge in a whirlwind. The baby stopped crying, his little mouth open. A moment later, a small dragon rested on Petar's palm. It wasn't alive like Amund, but it was a brilliant yellow and orange color from the stone.

Jarry clapped his hands and cooed.

"A dragon, huh? Nice trick, Maker."

"What can I say? I was inspired by our ... wedding gift." He exchanged a knowing glance with Usilea.

"Wedding gift?" Renna asked. Then her face lit up. "Do you mean—we heard rumors—it was the reason we didn't bring Opal, but—Abstephian dragons are supposed to be a myth."

Petar laughed. "My uncle thought it should be otherwise. As the Eternal would have it, Usilea and I are far better friends to Amund. Come, we will introduce you to him."

As they walked, Jaric fell into step beside him. For a moment, he watched his son play with the miniature dragon, which had been made with no sharp edges.

"He's going to try and eat that," he grunted.

"Neither the stick nor the rock are poisonous," Petar replied.

"Hm. I read Usilea's letter about how you two met a while ago. How she thought you were part of her mind."

Petar shrugged. "She is my closest friend. I would do anything for her."

"I gathered that, but good answer." He clapped Petar on the back. "Welcome to the family, Pet."

"Thank you, Jaric." He sighed, not even bothering to hide it.

"Now, if this dragon proves to be a hoax ..."

"You can see for yourself."

He halted in front of Amund's vessel. The large side doors were opened once again, and the scent of burning plants emerged. It was a testament to Amund's self-control that he had not set the entire ship ablaze.

"Open doors. Very impressive." Jaric's voice was flat.

Renna and Usilea joined them in front of the ship.

Come out, Amund. We have arrived at our new home.

There was a small, curious cry like a rusty gate, then the plant dragon slowly crept out of the hold, his wings tight against his sides. His head swiveled around, taking in the area from all angles, his claws scraping at the cement dock.

"Oh my ..." Renna breathed.

Jarry bubbled and squirmed.

Petar turned to Jaric, who took his son once more. His brother-in-law was grinning broadly.

"Finally, something to make this job more interesting." He glanced at Usilea. "You did well, sister."

"Our parents arranged the marriage," she replied with a smirk.

"Ah, let's not give them credit they don't need."

Usilea shook her head and moved up next to Petar, rubbing her hand in circles on his back. Warmth filled him.

"Have I told you that I'm grateful you aren't imaginary?"

He wrapped an arm around her shoulders.

I love you, too.

You offer the dreams and the safety of night

All cares and concerns

Vanished from sight

Yet beware, my dear

Of the thorns at sunrise

I say we are destined for goodness and joy

All madness and mayhem

Will never destroy

Though I know, my dear

There are thorns at sunrise

I claim we can stop that which is foul

All horrors and harbingers

No longer despoil

Yet remember, my dear

There are thorns at sunrise

We will try as we may

We will try as we might

To remove them

THORNS AT SUNRISE

Together

We will fight

Against the thorns at sunrise

A sacrifice made

A sacrifice lost

A victorious end

A justifiable cost

To regain what was lost

When the thorns

Came

At sunrise

Hey there! Thanks so much for reading.

Usilea's had a difficult life, so for this book I wanted some whimsy for her amidst all the doom. Also, I happen to be married to a teasing, self-sacrificing guy, so Petar was a delight to write on the page. And yes, I might have started drafting this book when my husband and I were in Covid quarantine from each other, and *sighs* I missed him! Text isn't the same.

Reviews are always appreciated!

If you haven't read *Met by Midnight* yet (Renna and Jaric's story), make sure to check it out! Their story is a retelling of Cinderella with a dystopian twist where a corrupt sanctuary takes the place of the wicked stepmother and stepsisters.
Plus, there's a wonderful labradoodle.
And a library.

And speaking of libraries, yes, Larkin is getting her own book and it will be a Beauty and the Beast retelling and it will involve books. Because clearly, the young woman enjoys books!

And for more exciting story news first, sign up for my email newsletter, Bookish Vibes.

And lastly, if you want to read more poetry, check out my Unique Words poetry collections.

Have a wonderful day!

ACKNOWLEDGEMENTS

Endless thanks to my Creator, for seeing in me what I could not see myself.

A massive hug of joy to my husband Stephen, a guy who I am very much a fan of being around.

All the gratitude to alpha readers Sarah Delena White, Hannah Wilson, Jessica Fry, Stars, and H.L. Burke for letting me spam your message boxes with story snippets (and giving honest feedback, even when I don't feel like adding more words).

Shout-out to fabulous beta readers Gretchen E.K. Engel, Lorelei Angelino, Jenelle L. Schmidt, and Kelly Thomas for giving of your time and attention. I really appreciate it and the story is better off.

Much thanks to editor Sarah McConahy for soldiering through another lyrical, five-line-sentences manuscript and for making sure that all the words actually make sense.

Massive amounts of gratitude to Yvonne Less at Art4Artists for the awesome cover design. So good!

Special thank you to Stars for pushing me in bravery with this story.

And finally, so much thankfulness to my faithful readers in both my reader group and scattered far and wide. You are amazing, and I hope this encourages you.

ABOUT THE AUTHOR

Janeen Ippolito believes that books change the world. She's the multi-published author of 20+ books, including bestselling fiction, nonfiction, and poetry. She's also an experienced editor and marketing strategist, and for seven years was the CEO of Uncommon Universes Press, a publishing company with award-winning books. Oh, and she hosts the Author Elevate Podcast, a book business and marketing podcast, and speaks regularly at conferences. In her spare time, she helps her epic husband with his youth swordfighting ministry, indulges her foodie ambitions, reads whatever she wants, and explores a slew of random hobbies. Her life goals include traveling to Antarctica and riding a camel while wearing a party hat. She loves to collaborate and encourage, so connect with her on social media or at janeenippolito.com

www.ingramcontent.com/pod-product-compliance
Lightning Source LLC
Chambersburg PA
CBHW030345180626
46812CB00007B/2761